FIRST BLOOD

First Blood
(Blood Rights, Book Six)

K. B. Thorne

This story is dedicated to my dog Jol, who was the best rescue pup that anyone could have ever asked for and one of the most special dogs to ever grace my life. There will never be a day where I don't miss him.

Cats & Dogs

Timeline: This story takes place after *Blood & Thunder*.

"Sadie, why am I here?" I leaned back against the bed of my New York City hotel room and stared at a very boring white ceiling with my cell phone on speaker above my head. I was there against my will. "I thought that bosses were supposed to *discourage* their employees from taking vacations."

"Perhaps they are," she replied, "but this boss happens to live with you, and she's tired of seeing you skulking around the house every Saturday night like a werewolf turned zombie."

I frowned, or pouted, really. "You aren't even home every Saturday night." I sounded petulant because I felt petulant. I wanted to be home and doing my job, but I'd been all but tossed onto the train and ordered not to come back until late Monday.

She didn't hesitate before replying. "I can feel you skulking at a distance." I opened my mouth to reply, but she shut me down. "Maddie, I'm a vampire and I have more of a life than you do! And weren't you just harassing me without mercy a couple of months ago to get out and live again? Cameron wouldn't want you hiding any more than me."

"I'm the only one who gets to use my brother like a talisman to beat people with," I muttered, but without venom. Sadie was practically my sister, and maybe if my brother hadn't been murdered like a dog in the street, she would have eventually become my sister by law and not just by heart. Still, she was happy now with her cat shifter cop boyfriend, and I was happy for her. And I was sure that wherever Cameron was, he was happy for her too. And finding lots of flaws in the cop, like the fact he was a cat.

"I have the cops watching the bus stations, train stations, and our house. If you show up before Monday night, I'm having them arrest you." She sounded like she really meant it, too. She had become quite the scoundrel lately.

I propelled myself to my feet. "Fine, I give!" I held up my hands in a surrender that I knew she couldn't see, but if she was as psychic as she claimed to be then I knew she'd know. "What do you want from me, woman?" I laughed, though. I couldn't help it. Cameron always said I had too much chipper deep down to be annoyed for long.

She knew I surrendered like I knew she was smiling. "A little love, Madison, is that too much to ask?"

I tugged my t-shirt over my head and yanked something dressier out of my backpack as I toed off my sneakers. "Right now?"

"I'm hanging up." She laughed, and the phone clicked. That was that. I was on vacation and on my own.

The clock read half past six. I had put on a salmon-colored cowl-neck that everyone said complimented my pale skin and hair, and I put on faux snakeskin high heels, but the blue jeans were going to stay. She could make me go on vacation, but she couldn't make me be uncomfortable.

With little other choice but to enjoy myself, I went down to the hotel bar. I had expected it to be busy for a Friday night, but not nearly filled with as much buzzing as it was. My senses—sight and smell and sound—far more sensitive than a human's, were overwhelmed in an instant, and I almost turned to flee. Somehow, I managed to overcome and walked in.

No sooner had I found myself a seat at the bar than I looked down the length of the room and saw the source of the commotion. There was a gaggle of women, and there really was no other word to describe the group, surrounding someone I couldn't see. Most of their backsides were barely covered by the shorts and skirts they wore, and I imagined their necklines were no less revealing, so clearly there was a man in the middle of the group and I guessed someone famous.

I admit I was curious, but there was no way I was going to get near that group, so I turned to the bartender and ordered a glass of Jack Daniels mixed with ginger ale. It was set down in front of me when a loud, incoherent exclamation came from the center of the estrogen maelstrom and they giggled, at first, before another sound followed that scattered them.

Now that they were gone, I had a chance to see who they had been flocking. My jaw dropped.

He was well over six foot. As a matter of fact, I knew he was 6'5" with reach in both his legs and arms. His hair was pure black and his eyes were a startling shade of orange-brown that no human would ever possess. With the girls gone, he was leaning against the bar, huddled around his glass and using his muscular shoulders to ward off anyone else.

That wasn't going to stop me. A giant emotional white cane hook swooped in from off-camera and forcibly yanked me down the length of the bar, sliding up beside him.

"My word, it's Chance Landry," I said, hopping onto the stool beside him. "Two hundred and thirty-seven pounds, second ranked in the newly created preternatural heavyweight class. I watched your last fight against Rodriquez."

He turned to look at me. It was a long look, his eyes starting at my hair before traveling down and back up again. It ended with a deep inhalation through his nose before he dismissively turned back to his drink. "You're a wolf."

I was undeterred. "And you're a cat." I knew that from his boxing stats, but also because I could smell cat all over him, and he radiated the power of a shifter, as well as the pronounced standoffishness of the feline group. I didn't mind. This wasn't a chance I would let slip by.

"Cats and dogs don't get along." He drained his glass.

"Well, they are supposed to be chasing each other. That's true," I granted. I took a long sip from my own glass and watched him.

He finally turned to look at me again. "To be fighting."

I grinned shamelessly. "Well, there are a lot of ways to… fight."

After a moment, he grinned. It was cocky and irrepressible. "Didn't you hear me send the other groupies running? You got a lot of nerve, wolf girl."

"You know, I get that a lot." He didn't scare me. I grew up in a pack of werewolves where girls were treated no differently than boys. We were all rough and tumble and balls and bravado. I offered my hand. "Madison St John."

He made a show of eyeing my hand before taking it, but he didn't change the way he sat. He just crossed one long arm over the other, but then I saw The Look. I had hoped to pass this by, but I made an occasion of his notoriety, so I guess I had to endure mine. "St John," he repeated the name, releasing my hand as connections formed in his brain. "Are you Cameron St John's sister?"

Holding back a sigh, I nodded. "I am."

From here, the reactions usually differed. Recognition seemed inevitable, but some people pitied me that my brother had been murdered just for being a werewolf and for daring to say we should be able to admit it, legally and safely. Some people liked to talk like they knew him, because he was in the news a lot, and they wanted to share opinions and recollections. Landry fell into the third category.

"Your brother had a set of brass ones, I'll give him that." Since he was looking into his glass when he said it, I might as well have guessed he was talking about his drink's brother, but I knew what he meant.

"Yeah, he did," I agreed. How could I not? Cameron had been the first one to stand up and say to the entire human world that the fiction freaks actually existed and not only that, you all should recognize us as not evil and as equal to you. And the craziest part was that he and Sadie, who was his girl at the time and dragged into it with him, succeeded! If only those hateful people hadn't killed him for it...

"You still here?" He was talking to me.

I blinked and chuckled. "Yeah, sorry." I shook my head to clear my mind. "You just got me thinking about Cameron. He was a great guy. I mean, he was a jerk, but I'm his little sister, so that's what I'm supposed to think. I just miss him."

This honest revelation apparently caught the boy by surprise and the man who, in the papers, was described as always having something to say seemed to be speechless, though it only lasted for a moment. "Need a refill?" He nodded at my glass.

Running my hand through my hair, I cocked my head to one side. "Am I allowed to stay, then?"

"Until you stop being interesting." That grin was back. He waved the bartender over and ordered us both a fresh drink, which was soon delivered as I took a seat beside him. I had no intention of becoming uninteresting, because quite frankly, I'm not. And I wasn't going to pass up the chance to hang out with one of my favorite sportsman.

I settled my elbow on the bar, my hand against my cheek. "Are you here promoting your book, that biography?"

He snorted. "That damn thing. Yeah, that's why I'm here. I didn't want to do it, but agreed to it just to shut my manager up. They thought it would be good for the sport, good for supernatural rights, and good for me. I don't know about the first or third, and don't care that much about the second. I mean, the legal shit is pretty good, but I'm not all that interested in being a crusader." It took him a minute to realize how that might come across and, contrary to his other conduct, he seemed to not want to let it hang there. "No offense."

"None taken. We aren't all meant to be…" I paused, looking for the word. "…instruments of social change."

"Did *you* want to be?" Those unique eyes watched me over the edge of his glass.

I laughed. "Are you kidding? I told Cameron he was nuts and that it wasn't going to do anything but get him either laughed out of school or killed, but he had it in him. He was passionate about it and brought the rest of us along with him."

He nodded and didn't say anything more. I wasn't thrilled with the direction of the conversation, admittedly, because too much of it could depress me, and I wasn't looking to be depressed tonight. I was under strict orders to enjoy my vacation, after all. I didn't know how to make a graceful turn off the subject, since it had dented my spirits.

"You want to go for a run?" His question startled me. Apparently, it showed. "You know, outside, running?"

I knew what he meant. No shifter could mistake the term. "We're in the middle of New York City. Where are we going to go for a run?" I laughed.

He got to his feet and pulled his jacket off the bar. His eyes were steady on me as he pointedly didn't answer my question, but that was answer enough, I supposed. He was challenging me. Suddenly, I felt as though my answer would prove the worth of werewolves everywhere, or condemn us.

Although no one likes to be challenged, I hated to feel

like I hadn't met one even more, so I got to my feet (whether stupidly or not is up to you to judge) and shrugged like I didn't care, when we both knew I damn well did. "Sure."

Whether I surprised him or not, I couldn't tell. But I knew he was pleased by my answer, and I felt a little pleasure at that. He paid for both our drinks, dropping bills on the counter like it was nothing, and slung an arm around my shoulders as we walked out.

Chance Landry was an arrogant bastard. There was no doubt at all about that. A guy who could get in the ring, both to take and give the beatings he did, kind of had to be. Was it stupid to leave the bar with a guy I just met? Probably, but like every other girl, I felt like I did know him, but I also knew I could take care of myself. Werewolf girls aren't like other girls.

Our hotel was in walking distance of the oft heard of Central Park, which was better for a run than I thought. I knew little of NYC and had only come here because it was close to Connecticut and seemed a good weekend spot, or so Sadie had said.

I'm going to rephrase that. I knew little of NYC and had only come here because Sadie said I should, and I think Vance had recommended it to her.

Once in the park and under the cover of darkness, it was remarkably easy to find a place in the trees to shift. We stripped out of our clothing with the natural lack of modesty typical in shifters, enough of the animal lives in us for that, although I caught his eyes running up and down my body a couple of times and I couldn't help but look at his well-defined muscular physique.

No sooner were our clothes and personal items stuffed under a crooked branch that would protect them—we were banking on—than we both threw ourselves into the transformation. It hurt like hell and always had. It always would. But it only took a few moments, some muscle snapping and joints popping, before I shook off the last feeling of my human form.

Few things are as liberating as standing in my beastly self. I wanted to howl at the moon but restrained myself. I don't know why. Maybe I didn't want to frighten the tourists.

Beside me, Chance stood in his massive tiger form. There could be little surprise at that. The animal form of a shifter is always bigger than a natural animal, and Chance was big as a human. He looked like a Siberian on steroids, but God Almighty, was he beautiful. And he knew it. He stood there all but preening for a moment before padding forward and bumping his big head into my shoulder in a surprisingly affectionate gesture.

After that moment, though, he head-butted me again with more force and knocked me one step to the side. I yipped a canine laugh as he took off into the trees and I chased him. After all, dogs were supposed to chase cats, right?

We must have been running for an hour inside the miracle of not seeing another soul, up close at least. There were others always at a distance, but it was impressive to be anywhere in NYC and have the chance to be alone and free in the refreshing, biting air. We chased each other. Sometimes, I was after him, and sometimes, he was after me. He always caught me before I could catch him. His legs were a lot longer than mine and so was his back. He had a huge, ground-eating stride.

I was getting a little too used to the freedom when I stopped short coming around a tree and seeing two people just on the other side of the park bench. The wind was against me, so I couldn't smell if they were human or not, but I could see and hear that neither of them were very happy. The words were indistinct, even to my hearing, but they were shouting.

Remembering it wasn't my business, I kept on my path and caught up to Chance as he loped between the trees. We ran for a while longer before finally returning to our clothes, where we happily found all of our possessions still there and exactly how we left them. Shifting back, we were reaching for our clothes when we heard an indignant squawk off to our left.

When I turned, I saw the woman that had been fighting with the man by the park bench. She now stood with a different man, and they had apparently wandered into our little spot to find us totally naked.

Neither Chance nor I were ashamed, but admittedly, I would rather have had my clothes on.

"Freaks," she shouted at us. "You have no business being in places where decent people are and doing…what you're doing."

I'd heard it before, or all sorts of variations on it. I didn't back down, but I wasn't going to get into a debate with her. She smelled human. And I knew LOHAV—or PAAS or whatever bigoted bullshit group she was from—when I heard it. This would need to be ended quickly.

"It's a free country, and we have every right to be as we are, which includes about our own business." I grabbed my clothes and started putting them on.

"It's too free by half. Freaks of nature should hardly be running around called citizens, let alone be allowed to be so offensive, naked in the middle of a public park with that gruesome shifting and the noise! It's indecent, and it's inhuman."

The man didn't say anything but wore the same contempt.

Chance growled beside me. "It is inhuman, 'cause we ain't human. We're better. Even some skinny-ass chick like you oughta be able to see that." He wasn't bothering to restrain himself, get dressed, or move on.

The woman smiled. It wasn't a pleasant smile. She

would have been pretty otherwise, I think, but there was a lot of blind hatred in that face. Only LOHAV attracted the really violent ones, the ones that looked at you like nothing more than a virus or a rodent and planned to knife you in an alley.

LOHAV—the League of Humans Against Vampires—had been more than a thorn in my side for a long time. They rose quickly enough during the legislation process, and they killed my brother and nearly my best friend. I hated them more than anyone or anything in my entire life, but I wasn't about to be arrested because of one of them. They weren't worth it.

Shirt in hand, I inserted myself between Chance and them. He was almost a foot taller and nearly that much broader through the torso and shoulders. I put my hand on his bare chest.

"Don't," I said in a low voice. He didn't look at me, staring over my head at the other woman. "Chance!" I shouted his name, and his head snapped down. He looked like he was about to give me the sharp side of his opinion, but something stopped him. I hoped it was me. "She's not worth it."

"You can't just let people talk shit to you like that." He wanted a fight. I could see it all over his face, and I was standing in his way. But I knew he could have just pushed me aside and hadn't.

"Sometimes, you gotta suck it up and take the hit." I used a phrase I hoped would break through the angry haze in those eyes. "Do you want to get arrested? You're a shifter, and she's a human. You go after her in anything but clear self-defense and you're screwed. Bad words do not equal self-defense. Forget her. She's a moron, and you're better than she is, so leave it and leave with me."

He didn't say anything for a while. His heart thundered against my palm as he breathed heavily, but he finally dropped his head. "Fine." He turned and grabbed his clothing, stuffing his long body into it.

"You should be running," the woman muttered. She wasn't quite as loud as she had been, knowing there was still a chance we'd jump at them—they were only humans—but she still couldn't resist getting a stab in. Bitch.

I felt Chance tense beside me, but I curled my hand around his arm and he let it go. I don't know how I got him to listen to me, honestly, but I'm glad he did. We left our clear patch in the trees in the opposite direction, and neither of the humans followed us.

"I should've pounded her right into the ground." His voice was low, but I couldn't miss what he said. I understood the impulse, but it was one no one could afford to indulge, least of all one of us. "Lucky for her that you were there, I guess."

I wondered if the fact that I'd stopped him lowered me in his opinion, but I couldn't afford to care about that any more than I could have gone after that woman.

Neither of us said anything else until we reached the hotel bar we had started in. In fact, neither of us said anything much after that either, other than ordering new drinks. We both felt like sulking in our own mental fogs, apparently, and having been reminded yet again of my dead brother, I couldn't exactly summon the will to open new lines of conversation.

Several drinks were thrown at our shifter constitution before Chance finally sighed. The vodka seemed to ease him and relax the tension in his shoulders.

"Why did you pull me off of her back there, anyway?" He didn't look at me. "I mean, what does it matter to you if I let loose on some narrow-minded bitch who's just out to get after me? After you too, by the way, in case you didn't notice."

"I didn't think you needed to be arrested today when she went screaming to the cops and to the press that some shifter was mean to her in the forest," I replied easily. "I work with Sadie Stanton. I live in Adelheid. We get our share of crap from the press and the anti-preternatural movements. I spend a lot of time sorting through calls about this. They start petitions online, spam Facebook and Twitter, and never let us alone—and I work at a business for and by people like us. We have gigantic bullseyes on our backs." I finished my whiskey. "You don't think it bothers the hell out of me and makes me think about the violence that's been done? I know better than many people, and you know I do, but you gotta take the high road sometimes and just leave it. Let them be stupid on their own."

Sighing, I brushed my hair back from my face and went on. "Haven't you ever heard the old lesson? Don't get into a fight with an idiot. They'll drag you down to their level and beat you with experience."

Now, he looked at me sidelong, and I saw a hint of his earlier smile. "Guess you're pretty smart, for a dog and all."

I laughed. "Bastard." He was a cute bastard, though, and I thought he wasn't quite the jerk he liked people to think he was. Or maybe he was. But he was a great boxer and handsome as hell and I saw no problem with enjoying my vacation, damn it!

"I was wondering when you'd notice." He pushed his glass away. "Got a mini bar in my room."

I knew what he was asking, and I smiled. "Sounds good."

☾○☽

Somewhere around 2:30, I woke up for no particular reason. Chance's long arm was slung over my waist, and he was sprawled out, taking up most of the bed.

It took a lot of human liquor to get a shifter buzzed, but you can do it if you're determined enough. The number of little empty bottles on the floor and nightstand showed just how determined we had been. I swallowed down a groan as my head throbbed.

Minus the headache, a good time had been had by all, but I was possessed with that sudden panic that happens when you wake up like this. Not that I had *a lot* of experience at it, thank you very much, but still. I slid out from his languid grasp and hunted for my clothing in what little dim light came from the moon through the window and the numbers in the alarm clock. He grunted and shifted a few times but seemed solidly asleep while I dressed and headed for the door.

I thought I heard him mumble something, like he was waking up, just as I made my escape and got into the hallway.

❨O❩

For no reason I knew, I woke up just after nine the next morning. My headache was gone, and I had a lingering memory of showering after I got back to my room before collapsing into bed and falling right back asleep. My body clock was all sideways, since I usually worked nights, so I didn't know what it thought it was doing, but I was awake at nine and there was no going back to sleep.

I still wasn't entirely sure why I felt the Walk of Shame at two in the morning had been necessary, but who can guess at the reasons for anything at that hour after the sort of evening I'd had?

Gazing longingly at the phone, I wanted to talk to Sadie, but it was light out and she'd be dead now. Kind of literally, but not really. Vampires were just confusing like that, but I didn't usually hold it against her. So, with that not being an option, I tossed myself out of bed and got dressed. I headed down to the dining room for my complimentary breakfast.

Not five minutes had I been seated when I saw a familiar pair of very long legs slide into my line of sight. I lifted my head and met his gaze. He looked more clear-sighted and awake than I did. How was that fair?

"Ain't cool you just takin' off like that." He sat down without being invited but smiled without any malice in his words. "Do I drool in my sleep or something?"

"No, but you snore."

"Do not."

"Sure, all cats do."

"No, all *dogs* do."

I laughed and drank my coffee. "I don't know why I took off, to be honest. I'm not really used to waking up naked in the beds of guys I've only known for a few hours. I think I just panicked." However, my usual humor was asserting itself and saving me from the awkward conversation this would have been if it had happened seven hours ago.

He shrugged. "No big deal." His plate looked like a heart attack waiting to happen with all that meat, but hey, he had a lot in the *I can survive eating Tupperware* category, so I wasn't going to say anything. "How long are you in New York for?"

"Doesn't that question usually come before the clothes come off?" I grinned. "I'm not here for long. I go home late Monday. I didn't really want to come, but my friend—who also happens to be my boss—said I had to, so I'm here."

"Sounds like me and my agent. I at least hope you don't have to sit through interviews and signings and mobs of idiot fans."

"No, we can safely say I avoid that." I poked a loose grape around my plate with a wedge of toast. "I don't have any plans other than to stay busy and try to relax, find ways to entertain myself until I can go home."

The full grin asserted itself. "Well, I'm here till Sunday night before I fly back to LA. My free time is yours till then."

That was an offer that was hard to pass up. "So, how

long do I have you for this morning?"

And we spent a surprisingly easy-going morning together. He didn't have anything till one, so we finished breakfast and went out about the city. When we weren't being harassed by stupid people, in one way or another, he was a fun guy to hang around and knew NYC a lot better than I did. He also had a lot of money and didn't mind spending it.

Okay, I know, it sounds awful of me, but I honestly tried to pay my own way on things. He wouldn't let me. And I'll confess it's nice to have that happen from time to time. I didn't abuse the privilege or anything. It was just a few drawing supplies at an art boutique and a nice lunch before we returned to the hotel.

It was in the hotel lobby that the day stopped being pleasant.

There were two men in suits talking to the man behind the counter. This wouldn't have stood out except that the concierge pointed to Chance and I as we walked in, and the suits immediately approached us. They flashed NYPD badges and very solemn expressions.

"Are you Chance Landry?"

Chance's body went rigid beside me. He nodded without saying anything, but his brow had knit into a deep V.

"We'd like to ask you to come to the station for questioning."

"What?" Chance looked at me, and I looked back. The look was unanimous: *what the hell?*

"Do you know this woman?" They showed us a picture, and we both instantly recognized her from the night before as the chick from the park, although she looked like she was dead on a morgue table in that photo. We said we recognized her. "She was found dead this morning in the stairwell of this hotel around ten. A witness said they witnessed you, Mr. Landry, threatening Ms. Reed last night in Central Park."

My mind jumped back to the short encounter. It could only be the man that was with her.

"We will need a statement from you as well." This was directed at me.

They drove us down to the precinct, and no one said anything on the drive. I didn't know what to think, except that I didn't think Chance had killed anyone. It was hard to argue with the fact he had been really upset in the park, but by morning... Well, we'd both felt a lot better.

We were split up as soon as we got there. I hadn't spent much time in police stations, let alone ones with the bustle of the NYPD. I'll readily admit I was overwhelmed and more than a little scared, but it was a fairly simple process with only a few questions. Apparently, I wasn't considered a suspect, so I told them about seeing the woman arguing with the man, but no, I didn't see him well enough to describe him, and yes, there was an altercation, but no, Chance didn't hurt her, and I was with him until very early this morning and then again later.

They didn't tell me anything, like when they thought the woman was killed, so I had no idea if I'd just helped or hurt his case.

I was driven back to my hotel alone after signing my statement, and they wouldn't tell me anything about Chance, but I didn't see him at the hotel. I called his room to no answer, so I guessed he was still there.

It was after four by the time I got to my room, and I didn't know what to do with myself. I had been down there for more than three hours, and Chance was still there. I had nothing to do but dwell for more than two hours. I couldn't concentrate on anything. I just kept waiting for him to come back, because I knew he would. He didn't do it... I didn't think he had. I mean, I had only known him for a day but still, I didn't think my senses and judgment were so badly impaired that I'd be so drawn to a murderer. I hoped not! If they were,

I needed therapy.

The minute it was dark, I was on the phone. I was practically vibrating around the room waiting through the rings and nearly had a stroke when it reached voicemail. I hung up without leaving a message and called back ten minutes later. This time, Sadie answered.

"Sadie! Oh God, I need your help."

"What's going on?" Her voice was all concern, with a dash of trying-to-wake-up.

The entire story just fell out in one giant, single-breath block of speech. She tried to tell me to slow down a few times but it didn't work, I just kept talking. When I was done, I was out of breath and panting.

She didn't say anything for a long moment before she finally cried, "I sent you on vacation! You are doing it *wrong*!" She calmed down after that. "Madison, I agree that it's awful, but I'm not sure what you want me to do about it."

"I don't know." I threw myself onto the bed. "You work with the cops. You date one. There must be something you can do or some kind of advice you can give me."

She laughed ruefully. "I wish that I could, but I can't. This has to do with people I don't know, except for you, and in New York City. I'm over here in little Adelheid. I have no magical powers over the Big Apple."

Idiotically, I wondered why people called it that. "Why not?" I sounded like a little kid, but didn't really care.

She was smiling sympathetically. I could tell. "How do you know they even think that he's a suspect?"

"Just seems obvious. He's been down there for questioning forever, and they said they had a witness that he threatened the victim hours before she turns up dead. I mean, it's pretty obvious to me."

"I don't mean to hurt your feelings, but I do have to ask: how do you know that this guy is innocent, anyways? You know him from television and the past twenty-four hours." I heard the fridge opening and closing in the background at our house.

"I don't know," I admitted. "I just do. You get feelings about people, and I'm pretty good about it. I don't think he's the kind of guy who'd do something like this, and before anyone can say he beats people up for a living, I'll point out that I think it could make him less likely to because he gets that alpha male shit out of the system in a scheduled way rather than letting it build up and explode." I forced myself to stop and take a breath. "I'm sure he's innocent."

"Then I am sure he is, too. Just do me a favor, okay?"

"What's that?"

"You've got that tone in your voice that says you're stuck on something. I don't want you to go all Nancy Drew on this and get in the cops' way if you think they're wrong." Now, she sounded more like a mother than a friend.

I'll admit it hadn't come as any conscious thought, but there was that lingering feeling underneath that wanted to do something. I think it was just sitting still for too long without knowing anything. "Nancy Drew solved all her cases, though," I had to point that out.

She sighed. "She was also a fictional character, dear. I don't want to be bailing *your* non-fictional ass out of jail for obstruction and just being stupid."

"They can put you in prison for that now?"

"You're going to kill me. I'm already dead, but just being associated with you is going to kill me a second time. Just... be smart, okay? Hopefully, your guy there will come back and say it's all fine, and it will be. Just take deep breaths and don't jump out any windows."

I sighed. "I'll do my best."

"*Madison...*"

"I promise!"

After hanging up with her, there was still no sign of Chance. I called his room again, but there was no answer, so I went to it just to give myself something, anything, to do. I sat outside the door like a woman who'd lost her key.

It was around 7:00 when he came back, and he brought thunderclouds with him. I jumped up. "What happened?" I asked without preamble. He didn't answer me as he opened the door and for a moment, I thought he was going to blow past and lock me out, but as soon as he stepped inside, he waited and held the door open till I was in.

"They think I killed her!" It was out as soon as the door clicked shut. "They didn't have enough to hold me, but it was pretty damn clear that they think I did it."

"What do they know about what happened?" I sat on the edge of his bed and watched him pace the length of the room. It had seemed like a very big room last night, and now it seemed like it couldn't possibly be big enough.

He ran his hands through his hair. "They think she bought it a little after four this morning, which means I don't exactly have an alibi."

Not that he said it with animosity, but I winced anyways. "I wish I hadn't slipped out."

"I wish you hadn't either." He snorted, bringing to mind an angry bull more than a cat, but then he sat down hard on the bed beside me. "She was beat to hell and tossed down a couple steps, enough to kill her. Their witness has me threatening to pound her into the ground. I didn't think whoever that idiot with her was could have heard that, but I know that you weren't giving any statements after ten this morning unless you can be in two places at once."

"Thanks for the vote of confidence."

"Give me a break here, damn."

"Sorry."

He cracked his knuckles. "They don't sound like they

have much more than that, but I don't get the idea they have anyone else."

I frowned. "What about the guy I saw fighting with her?"

"I don't know. I didn't see him, and they didn't say anything else about it. But they were working me pretty hard. I got a bit of a reputation, you know? But, I called my lawyer. I have a few of them, so they damn well better earn the ridiculous retainers I pay them, and they didn't hold me. I practically have a straitjacket on till they sort this shit out, and who knows when that will be."

I put my hand on his leg. "I'm sure they'll get it sorted out and this will all be cleared up." It was an empty platitude, and we both knew it, because what did I know?

In silence, we sat like that for a while. Finally, he asked if he could have some time alone, and I left. I didn't like it, but I got it. Tigers are solitary. Wolves are pack. When I'm upset, I want to be around people. I guessed when he was upset, he didn't. I couldn't force my company on him because *I* was bothered.

So, I went back to my room, but I didn't stay there very long. In fact, I went right back out to do exactly what I'd promised Sadie I wouldn't.

If you're wondering why I was on such a tear to prove the innocence of a man I barely knew who hadn't yet actually been arrested for a crime, then you'd be asking yourself a very good question. I was asking myself the same thing. I didn't have an answer either, although I think it had something to do with Cameron. I'm not sure how, but it did.

That's why I went down to the front desk. The guy on duty was the same one I'd seen there when I left the bar the second time with Chance. He looked like he recognized me as I walked up and was immediately suspicious.

"Hi," I said, because I really didn't know how one did this.

"The cops already talked to me."

I frowned. Was I that obvious? "How did you know what I was going to ask you?"

He shrugged. "I'm paid well to guess what people are going to want, and I could just tell, after seeing you with him. You look like the curious type."

I wasn't sure how to take that. "Well, you talked to the cops, so there's no reason that you can't talk to me. I just want to figure out what's going on."

"That seems like the kind of thing the cops wouldn't want you doing."

I knew he had a point. I knew Sadie had a point. I knew that I should listen to them. It wasn't like Chance had asked for my help. In fact, he'd kicked me out. Still, I couldn't seem to help myself.

So, I smiled in my cutest and most pathetic way. "Can't you throw me just a little bone?" I asked, which—from a werewolf—I knew sounded strange, or fitting. "I just need to understand, so can you help me out just a little?"

It took him a moment, but he relented. "Only because you remind me of my sister," he murmured. After taking a quick look around, he leaned toward me. "I saw the woman here in this lobby around two-thirty this morning, not long before I got off work. She didn't look very happy and had me call her a cab to McNally's, which I did. I went off work at three and didn't see her again."

"Thanks," I said with a big smile of appreciation. Part of my brain wondered if I should give him money, but as I was entirely inexperienced at this, I hoped my gratitude would suffice and headed out to the street.

Much like ants crawling through an ant farm, the streets of New York were filled with yellow taxicabs. I flagged down the first one I could and told them to take me to McNally's, which turned out to be a bar in a building's basement. The sign was in green with gold-painted engraving, and I got a distinct pub feeling when I walked in, which was cool.

Having no clue at all what I was looking for, I took a seat at the bar.

I ordered a whiskey, which seemed to please the bartender, and then just sat and thought and listened.

This plan served me well, because before long, my werewolf hearing caught tidbits of a low-spoken conversation behind me being held in a booth just a little to my left. I only picked up pieces of it through the din of the rest of the bar, but it was enough to intrigue me.

"...I told you not to get physical. Why don't you ever listen to me when I..."

"...wasn't supposed to happen that way. She got upset and pushed and..."

"...cops said she was beat to hell before she was pushed off..."

"...Reed started it. I can't be blamed..."

"...you are not listening to me now! She was beaten. I can't see it a fair fight when..."

I swallowed my whiskey in one shot and paid for my drink. As he brought my card back, I glanced over my shoulder to see the two men, hunched over their drinks. I saw the back of one and the face of the other. I kept my look quick, because I didn't want them to know that I had seen them.

Slipping outside, I paused on the sidewalk and tried to figure out exactly what I planned to do with this information. I should have thought of this before, I realized, but I couldn't exactly go to the cops and say I'd done what they would not have wanted me to do, if they even believed it.

The street was so full of sounds and scents that I didn't realize I had been followed until an arm dragged me against the wall. It was the man from the booth!

He had me in a shadow, the space between lights, with

a hand against my mouth. I didn't know what to think or do at first, I was so startled. "What do you think you're doing?" he demanded. "Spying on me and my mate?" If he expected an answer, he wasn't going to have much luck with my mouth covered. He didn't smell like a shifter, but there was still something powerful about him that made me evaluate my chances.

His eyes narrowed. "You were with Landry. I wouldn't be around that one too much." He smirked. "You stay out of my business. I don't know what your game is, but I don't care. If I see you again, I'll make you regret it. Understand?"

I nodded. I thought I could take him, being a shifter and all, but if I could get out of this without having to fight anyone. Maybe that was better. Besides, I was kind of scared out of my wits. He favored me with one last sinister look before stalking off. Very briefly and stupidly, I considered following him, but I decided against it.

Chewing a hole in my bottom lip instead, I got a cab back to the hotel.

Chance was outside my room when I got there. I stared wide-eyed at him. He was stalking back and forth in front of the door until he saw me and stalked up, getting in my face. Or staring down in my face.

"Where the hell have you been?" He threw an arm in the air over his head. "With all this shit, I would have thought that you'd stay put, and then I was down at the front desk, and he mentioned you were asking questions? I know you like me and all, but do you really want to end up in a jail cell with me?"

I gaped and couldn't think of a single thing to say.

He looked like he was about to let loose another tirade but then stared in my eyes a moment too long. "What's wrong?"

I didn't *want* to tell him, he would just yell at me some

more, but I did anyways because secret-keeping hasn't always been my best ability, except in certain situations. This moment wasn't one of them. I told him what I did.

Chance's broad shoulders swelled with a deep breath, like he was going to bust open again, but then he pointed at the door. "Inside."

Chastised, I unlocked the door and let us in.

"What is wrong with you?!" The expected explosion came right after we shut the door behind us. "Are you crazy? You could have been hurt! This guy might have killed that woman, and you go following him around? Alone? God, damn, wolves really are nuts." He was pacing again.

Instead of trying to defend myself, because I couldn't really find a way to do that, I got the art supplies we had bought that morning—seemed longer ago than that—and began sketching. Chance ranted for a while longer before dropping to a seat beside me. "What are you doing?"

I drew a hair line. "I'm drawing the man that threatened me."

"Really? I didn't know you could do that." He leaned into me, peering at my sketchbook as I worked. I didn't say anything but let the face emerge. The image was burned into my mind so recently that it didn't take much work for the face to come out.

When I was done, I looked at it and frowned. "I think this might have been the guy I saw her fighting with in the park last night."

He frowned now, too. "We have to show this to the cops."

"And say what?" I tossed it back on the bed. "They'll probably not even believe me because they'll say I'm trying to defend you. If they do believe me, I will be in trouble for getting in the way."

"You probably should have thought of that before you went Hardy Boys."

"I'm a girl. I'd be Nancy Drew."

"You can be Jessica Fletcher for all I care! It was a dumbass thing to do."

I looked at him with surprise. "You know who Jessica Fletcher is?"

Looking embarrassed, he got to his feet. "Yes, I used to watch *Murder, She Wrote* with my grandpa, okay?" He rubbed the back of his neck. "I'm going to go get us a drink. Stay here and don't do anything else stupid, all right?"

"I'll try." I smiled. He looked unimpressed, and a little worried, but left the room.

Honestly, I had really meant to stay put and behave. But I looked at the picture and had a thought occur to me. I wouldn't leave the hotel this time, so I'd be fine. I ripped the sheet off the notebook, folded it, and put it in my pocket. Leaving the room, I meant to be down to the lobby and back up before Chance was.

Unfortunately for me, the elevator in this section was out of order, so I took the stairs rather than go to the other end of the hallway. I think I went this way to avoid Chance, just in case.

About two stories down, I realized there was someone walking up. As the elevator was out, this wasn't a surprise. What was a surprise was when I saw the face from the drawing in my pocket walking toward me. Our eyes met.

"Shit," I said and then didn't even bother to see if he had any explanation. I turned and bolted because I did not want to get into a fight.

I heard his heavy steps pursuing me, and he was a lot faster than I expected. Despite my advantage, I only made it up a half-flight before he caught me and pushed me forward. I caught myself on my hands against the top step. Scrambling onto it, I lunged for the door, and he caught me by the hair.

That just pissed me off, and I spun around with my

elbow flying. He caught it right in the nose and shrieked like a girl, pressing his hands over the flowing blood. I bulled past him and ran downstairs now. Remarkably, I heard him chasing me again, though with a great many curses to tell me where he was.

Reaching the next floor, I was moving too fast to catch the door. I slid on my heels to turn and grab it, but before I could, it opened and Chance stepped in, clothes-lining the guy and knocking him on his ass before the weretiger's big hands had him by the jacket front and was holding him against the wall. Chance's arms were much longer. And the tiger looked only too pleased by the idea of tearing this guy apart, if for no other reason than he was lacking a better option of where to vent his frustration. He growled quietly, low in his throat.

"You might want to call the cops, sugar," Chance said.

⦅○⦆

I sat in the NYPD Station with Chance at my side. He wasn't happy with me. The cops weren't happy with me. Sadie and Vance weren't going to be happy with me. Still, everyone had grudgingly acknowledged my help after the thug confessed to killing Penny Reed in an argument over a gambling debt.

Fortunately, Chance was off the hook, and I wasn't going to be arrested for obstruction or being stupid. We were just waiting for the last paperwork to sign before they let us go.

"Are you heading back to LA tomorrow still?" I asked, gripping the edge of my seat and leaning forward. I felt a little like a kid waiting in the principal's office.

"Yeah," he agreed. "Too bad this weekend couldn't have turned out differently."

That was hard to argue with. "Do you come out much to the East Coast? I'd like to see you again, without the murder and cops." I smiled at him.

He chuckled, dropping an arm around my shoulders and making me lean back. "I get out this way from time to time. When I do, I'll definitely be looking you up."

"Good."

"And if your boss ever makes you vacation in LA, give me a call." He grinned that grin as he stuffed a napkin down my cleavage.

They called him in then, and I was left alone in the waiting area, pulling the napkin back out. I sighed, but my phone rang and gave me something more to do. "You're lucky you're not in jail. Did you not listen to a single thing I said the past two days?" Sadie wasn't pleased with me, but I knew she loved me anyways.

I laughed apologetically. "I did, but things just didn't go as expected."

"I told you to take a vacation and get some rest. To enjoy yourself, not solve murders."

"I know, but you know," I said, staring at Chance's phone number and grinning because nothing could hold me down for long, and then looked through the squad room and saw Chance on the other side. "I kind of had fun."

Family Matters

Timeline: This story also takes place sometime after *Blood Moon.*

I couldn't get rid of my fucking brother.

Not that I was trying to kill him or something. I'm a bitch and have been called psychotic on more than one occasion, but I'm not *that* bad. Besides, after centuries without him, I was happy he was back in my life. I just had never imagined that having him in my life meant he would be in *every single corner* of it, even my work, which is really more of a solo endeavor.

My name is Dakota. I work for the Stanton Agency as a bounty hunter. Cameron's Law has made all preternaturals, like me, legal citizens, but sometimes, they still go wrong and when they do, they call me. I catch the scary ones. I catch the ones that no one else can, because I'm scarier than they are.

I'm a theriomorph. We are so rare that I only know of two still alive: my brother and myself. There had been my sister, but she kind of turned out...wrong and had to be put down. Don't ask. I don't like talking about it, but the good thing was that my brother found me.

The bad thing was that my brother found me. And I couldn't get rid of him. He followed me everywhere, and since he has the same abilities to change into any creature or any human form he wants, like I can, he is the only creature alive that *can* follow me.

"Stop telling me how to do my job!" I shouted at him in the middle of the Stanton Agency's office. The agency served the preternatural community, but they couldn't really serve anyone while Eddie and I were screaming in the front office.

"Why do you have to be such a menace to society?" he asked, throwing his hands in the air. "I don't get why you're doing a job that serves the public when you obviously can't stand the public."

We'd had this argument before.

"I get to hunt the public in this job, and I like that." I shifted my vocal cords, making a rattling hiss.

He returned it with a deep growl. I think it was a bear. It was his favorite form.

"Children!"

"What?!" both of us shouted, our heads snapping around to look at Madison. She was a werewolf who ruled over the agency's office. She works the night shift, which is when most of the agency's business is done. (The day secretary is a glorified answering machine, really.) Madison was also practically the sister of the boss, so she got to rule with an iron fist. Sometimes, that included us.

"How many times do I have to tell the two of you not to fight in the office? You have an apartment, Dakota. Please take your squabbles there." Madison had her manicured hands laced together, resting her chin on them. With her blue eyes and blonde hair, she looked like any Midwestern cheerleader, but I knew she had a wolf inside and wouldn't put up with our shit.

Eddie and I exchanged a glance and then looked away. "I'm sorry, Madison," we said in unison.

She was about to reply when the phone rang. Answering it, I turned and was going to leave when she whistled for my attention and I turned back. I listened to her side of the conversation.

"Why haven't you called the police, sir? I see. All right, yes, we do have someone who should be able to help you. Can you come down to the office? Great. Right now is fine." Madison met my eyes. "In fact, our hunter is here now. You can meet her right away. All right, good, we'll see you when you get here."

"What?" I asked, narrowing my eyes at her.

"Don't go away after all, but you still have to stop fighting in my office." She smirked. "You've got a possible client coming in who wants to hire you to find someone."

This smelled wrong, though I didn't have enough information to put my finger on anything. "Isn't a missing person the cops' area?"

Madison shook her head. "Not this one, but I'll let him explain. I know you don't like your office, but why don't you go sit in it? I'll direct him to you when he gets here."

Grunting, I walked down the hallway. After a few steps, I realized that Eddie was behind me. I turned. "Haven't you had enough of me yet?"

"Yes," he replied dryly, "but I have to make sure you play nice."

I opened my mouth and took a deep breath to reply, but a warning bark from Madison made me shut it again. I headed into my neglected office and tried to slam the door before Eddie could get in, but I was too slow.

Once inside, however, I didn't know what to do with myself. I really never used this room. I sat behind the desk. Tapped my boots on the floor. Avoided meeting my brother's eyes before I got another lecture on my attitude.

It had been decades since I had family, and it was taking a lot of getting used to, having someone getting on my case I felt compelled to listen to. I couldn't admit to *him* that I was actually listening, of course, and I wouldn't have minded having a little less to listen to.

Amazingly, he didn't say anything. Soon, there was a knock on the door. Madison let a man in, made quick introductions and then ducked back out. Edward stood behind me after gesturing for the client to sit.

This felt damned odd. Suddenly, I didn't know where to start, but a subtle kick to the base of my chair got me going.

"Mr. Winters," I began, forcing a tiny smile to keep Eddie from smacking me, "I understand that you have someone you would like me to locate?"

"Please, call me Charles."

He perched on the edge of his chair like a nervous bird, although there wasn't anything 'bird-like' about him. Unless you meant a penguin. He was a short, rotund little fellow with gray hair fringing his head and pink cheeks. He was very human and sweating profusely, apparently nervous, which poked at the inside of my preternatural nose, but I managed to ignore it.

"Mrs. Lucas is missing," he went on after a moment. He had a hat gripped between both hands, fingers digging in the squashed rim as he anxiously spun it in a circle. "I need you to find her."

"Why haven't you gone to the police?" I asked. It wasn't that I cared about the law all that much, but I had some people on the force I could almost call friends and didn't need to land my own ass in prison.

"I did," he said, a little indignantly, but it passed quickly. "They said that they couldn't do anything for me." Now, he looked distraught. I was going to need a flowchart to keep up with the moods. "There was a detective nearby who said that you could find anyone or anything."

That had to be Vance. Vance Johnston was a detective for the Adelheid Police Department, a weretiger, someone I almost called friend, and was dating the owner of the agency, Sadie Stanton.

Still, there was something odd here. "Was it too soon to file a report?"

"No, it's been almost a month."

Fishy, fishy... "Can you tell me a little about Mrs. Lucas, then?"

He paused, taking a shuddering deep breath before pulling a handkerchief from the pocket of his tweed suit to blot his brow. "She's middle-aged and has a bad leg, short and rather round. Her hair is short and fawn-colored." As he spoke, that twitching feeling between my shoulder blades began. "She has big eyes, far apart, and black ears. A kind of dome-like head..."

I held up a hand to stop him. "Is Mrs. Lucas a dog?" I asked carefully.

Charles frowned. "Didn't I say that?"

Just barely, I managed to avoid dropping my head. "No, you didn't."

"Oh, well, dear, yes, I should have clarified that. Mrs. Lucas is a dog. She's a Pug, and I adopted her at the shelter. She's been with me for only a few months but has really become a part of my life. I'm just sick with worry. See, my house was broken into, and the door was left open. It's only luck that I wasn't home at the time, but Mrs. Lucas vanished that night and I haven't seen her since. I told the cops then, but they said there wasn't much they could do."

I'd heard enough. "I'm sorry about your dog, but I—" Edward's hand was suddenly on my shoulder with a preternatural strength that matched my own. Partway to standing, I was forced back on my ass. I grunted but tried not to let on that I was being manhandled by my big brother in my own office.

Glancing up, I saw that he was smiling. "We'd be happy to help, Mr. Winters."

I gave him what I thought was a very clear *what the fuck*

do you think you're doing look, but he ignored me. Bastard.

Charles Winters practically beamed as he bounced to his feet and reached across the desk to shake our hands. "I'll pay whatever your fee is, if you can just find my dear Mrs. Lucas," he said. I gave him my hand because I knew Edward would make me if I didn't, but grabbed it back at the first chance so Winters was left shaking Eddie's far more enthusiastically.

"We'll need more information," Eddie continued, since this sure as hell wasn't going to be my job. I wasn't a Pug catcher. "May we come to your house? Since that was the last place she was known to be, that will be a good place to start."

"Of course, of course," Winters replied. "I'll be home all night. Come as soon as you're able."

"We'll be there in an hour," Eddie said. "Please just leave your contact information with the secretary out front."

Looking far more relieved than when he came in, Winters bounced out to the front office. I waited until the door shut before I grabbed Eddie's hand from my shoulder and yanked him forward, slamming his hand against the desktop. I slid to the side, wrenching his arm behind his back and driving his face-down.

He grunted and cussed, but I had him firm. "What the fuck do you think you're doing?" I hissed. "I don't do these kinds of jobs."

"It wouldn't kill you to act like a human being sometimes," he replied, sort of. It was hard to speak clearly with half his mouth against an unused desk blotter. "You don't have any other cases right now, the man's in pain, and this would be a good chance to exercise the part of you that doesn't see light much."

"Doesn't it occur to you that it doesn't see light much 'cause I want it that way?" I smooshed him a little harder against the desk, just because I could.

"Of course I know that," he grunted. "That doesn't mean

you're *right* to do it."

Suddenly, the heel of his boot collided dead center with my shin. I shouted something incoherent and let him go, hopping back. He was in front of me in the blink of an eye, smashing his forehead into mind and sending me reeling into the far wall.

"*Gott im Himmel*," I cried, clutching my forehead. "You've got a fucking hard head."

He started laughing. I looked up, glowering at him from under my hand, but then I had to start laughing too.

❰❍❱

In less than an hour, we were at the house of Charles Winters. I knew as soon as I had the address that this guy had a lot of money. There is one area of Adelheid where the cost of houses far outpace everywhere else in the town, and that was where this guy lived.

I parked my old SUV in front of his large brick home. Brick could be uncommon in the northeast, but it fit the wealthy feel. If I was a different kind of person, one prone to being self-conscious and giving a fuck what other people thought, I might think my car was out of place. As it was, the most I cared was in not locking it. With the types of cars at these houses, who'd want to steal my piece of shit?

My brother and I walked up to the front door and knocked. We were greeted by Mr. Winters himself, which surprised me. I'd expected a maid or a butler. He shook our hands warmly and bustled us into the living room, waving at the elegant sofa and offering us drinks.

"We're fine, thank you," Eddie said before I could say anything. He probably worried that I'd be rude, but the truth was, the solicitousness of the man was actually making me feel kind of bad for him. He was so sad about the loss of his dog that he was ridiculously grateful we'd be helping him. I would never admit my feelings to Eddie, but I kind of even *wanted* to help now. I wanted to find his dog for him.

I wasn't quite as heartless as people thought. I just couldn't afford to let them know that.

"I'm not sure how much you know about us," I began, jumping in to do my job, "but we're not human. We're theriomorphs, so we can change into all sorts of animals."

He was nodding quickly. "Yes, I read about you in the papers." He had to be in his sixties, but his eyes made him look really young and eager. It kind of unnerved me.

"Right," I said with a slow nod. "Well, what we're going to do is turn into dogs, and we're going to follow the trail." Eddie was watching me strangely, like he was shocked I knew how to be half-decent. "So we need you to show us where your dog spent the most time."

"Of course." Winters was on his feet before another word could be said, gesturing us to follow him. He led us into what appeared to be a second living room and showed us an elaborate corner with a purple dog bed, water dish, and a bunch of toys.

"I think this dog owns more stuff than I do," I murmured.

"Do you need anything else?" Winters asked, looking between the two of us.

I managed the barest of smiles as I shook my head. "This should do it. We'll just, you know, do our thing and see where it leads us." My senses, even in human form, were above average, and I had already picked up on something odd. I looked at Eddie, and he nodded. We both morphed into hounds, and I caught a glimpse of Winters' shocked face, because even if you knew we could do it, *seeing* it was always another matter.

Turning to the doggie Taj Mahal, Eddie and I didn't even need to put our noses to the ground to know that something wasn't right. This wasn't a dog we were smelling, at least not a real one. I did put my nose down, taking the scent in more deeply to my human/hound brain. It was barely familiar, like something you had only ever smelled once or twice and could remember but distantly.

It was going to poke at my brain until I figured it out. To keep the thoughts rolling, I followed the strange trail all over the house. Eddie followed me and Winters trailed behind, sometimes opening doors when we'd pause at them, and being shockingly well behaved. Most humans pelted us with questions, even knowing our mouths couldn't answer them. He was silent and just helped us along.

In the kitchen, I picked up a second scent. It was close enough to the first that I knew it was the same species, but different enough to be a different person. After a moment, I returned to human and turned to my employer. "Does anyone else live here with you?"

He shook his head. "No, it was just me and Mrs. Lucas." He smiled a little. "I named her after the character in *Pride & Prejudice*."

I thought it had sounded familiar.

"Do you have any frequent visitors?" I asked next. Eddie didn't bother to switch back, so he just sat beside me and listened. I was tempted with thoughts of putting a muzzle on him but knew he could just morph out of it. "Anyone who would be in the kitchen?"

Again, he shook his head. "Things had been disturbed in here after I discovered the break-in, though. Maybe you're smelling that person?"

Something, again, sounded just a little off. "Was anything taken?"

He shrugged. "Just my dog. Things were a bit of a mess, but she was the only thing gone. I tried to tell the police, but since I never received a call for money, they didn't think the dog was the point. But nothing else was taken, so I don't know what it could've been. The kitchen door here had been left open, so maybe she escaped... I don't know." He sighed and even his pink rotund cheeks seemed to sag.

"We're going to track out the door, then. If the trail continues outside, we may be gone for a little while, but we'll report in before we leave," I told him.

Eddie looked at me with a canine 'wtf?' look, but I just glowered at him briefly before returning to my dog form and joining him as we nosed our way out of the kitchen and into the well-manicured yard, where the second scent became more pronounced and the first scent faded. My first thought was that a Pug is small and probably was carried, maybe even put in a bag. If Mrs. Lucas had just run off, her scent would be stronger.

It vanished at the road, however, maybe into a car.

Pausing, I sat down and stared along the blacktop. The scent was strong in my nose, and my brain furiously tried to figure out what it was and where I recognized it from. I dealt in mysteries for a living but couldn't stand the little ones where the only reliable source was my own brain and that wasn't being so reliable.

Eddie started nudging me with his nose, but I ignored him while I thought. It finally came to me right as I was about to bite my brother: fae.

A memory from a couple of years back sprang to mind. Fae were odd creatures and could be rare to actually meet, but I'd met one. The scents were alike, and I knew that some fae could change their forms.

Without acknowledging Eddie, I turned and headed back to the Winters house.

☾O☽

I had kept my follow-up with Charles Winters short, because I didn't want to build false hope or give information that might be wrong. It just wasn't my style. There was more needing to be done before I could say anything for sure, but I had the odd idea forming that Winters had a fae for a pet. What I couldn't figure out was *why*. Fae tended to be enigmatic, but generally also vain and/or proud. Why would any fae want to spend time as someone's pet Pug? It just didn't make sense.

On the way home, I kept ignoring Eddie. It drove him nuts, which was why I did it.

It didn't matter to me that he'd been right about taking this case. In fact, that just made it worse. No one liked a know-it-all, right?

Back at the apartment, Eddie went off in a huff, and I settled in at my 'desk' to do a little work. My "office" was really just my dining room table, crammed in the open empty space between the kitchen area and the living room area of my studio apartment above a Chinese food restaurant. Even with Eddie staying with me, I kept my usual hovel because I happened to like it. Theriomorphs could sleep anywhere and in any form, so I just let him figure out his own sleeping arrangements. Sometimes, that meant he was unobtrusive as a human on the couch or a mouse in a corner. Other times, he decided to annoy me by sleeping as some house pet at the foot of my bed.

Picking up my cell phone, I called the police station and asked for Vance. I was connected a few minutes later.

"Dakota, this is a…surprise." I could tell he was smirking. "What can I do for you?"

I explained the situation to him as succinctly and not-smart-ass-ly as I was capable of, because I was asking for his help. He was quiet for a little while and then replied. I could practically hear him nodding as he spoke. It was odd how I could do that, because I wasn't used to knowing people that well.

"Yeah, I remember that case. I'm not in robbery, but this is too small a station to not hear things, and it was kind of odd. A dog-napping? Especially one that we couldn't even be sure was a dog-napping?" He shook his head, I could tell. "But what was weirder was that it struck a memory from some other reports of break-ins where a Pug dog was missing afterward. Those were different, though, because in those cases, it was a home invasion with a death. The owners were killed during the commission of the crime."

Now that sounded ominous. I wondered if there was a connection. Break-ins weren't unique enough to be a tie-in alone, but the missing dog thing was conspicuous.

"What can you tell me about those?"

Vance inhaled deeply. "Not all that much, really," he said. I heard computer keys tapping in the background. "The houses were broken into; we found broken windows at each one. The owners were all wealthy and had security, but the burglar was gone before emergency response arrived. In each one, the victims were men, single, in their forties to sixties, wealthy, owners of a Pug dog that was missing after every home invasion, along with many valuables. There are about three of these cases, each one a couple of months apart from the other. Perpetrator is still at large and with no leads."

"When was the last one?"

"A couple of months ago."

Something poked at the back of my brain, but I wasn't sure what it was. "Thanks, Vance," I said, distracted by the inner prodding.

"Let me know what you find out, would you?"

"Sure thing." We hung up.

In my distraction, I forgot to annoy my brother. He walked back into the area and crossed his arms over his chest. "Are you talking to me again yet?"

Without responding to that specifically, I instead

revealed what Vance had told me. Eddie got the same thoughtful look as me and sat down on the sofa, leaning back silently. I knew he was trying to figure out the connection the same as I was. I also told him about my suspicion that the scents belonged to a pair of fae. It only made his brow draw more strongly inward.

Neither of us said anything for a while, until Eddie finally said, "I just don't know."

"Makes two of us," I replied, going to sit next to him. Well, I'm not sure 'sit' was the appropriate description. It was more like I collapsed next to him. I shifted as I fell, shrinking my usually 6' body to a 5' frame that would fit better on the couch with another person there. "We need to know more about fae is what we need."

"You have any ideas where we can find that?" he asked.

"We could go talk to Sadie. I mean, she seems to know everything about anything when it comes to the preternatural community." I sat up just enough to look out the window then slumped back down. "It's dark out. She'll be in the office. Madison rarely lets her off the leash anymore."

"The secretary with the iron fist," Eddie quipped.

Although I found my couch very comfortable, and I was oddly tired, I sat up and then stood. "Let's get down there and see if Sadie can help us."

His eyes followed me. "Hot on the case, huh?"

I wondered briefly what that was a jab about, but I elected to do what I usually did when it came to conversations that could potentially be a Big Something: I ignored it. I just headed out of the apartment and let him catch up with me. And then I ignored him for most of the drive to the agency. Was it childish? Sure, but siblings had a way of bringing that out in each other. I had a feeling it was worse for us because the last time we'd spent so much time together, we'd been fourteen. So we were still trying to learn how to act like adults around each other. As I'm sure anyone who saw us could tell, it was slow-going.

At the office, I asked after Sadie, but she was busy with a client. I sighed and turned to find D sitting on the front office couch.

D was...interesting. Still a semi-new vampire. He refused to tell any of us (but Sadie) his real name. His job was basically to bodyguard the agency animator on the job, because she tended to get harassed by the anti-preternatural groups when she was animating the dead. He also did some IT work. He could be grumpier than I was when on his own, but not when his girlfriend Cassandra was around. He was the most collected guy in the world then, concerned only with protecting her, but she was quite the odd duck herself.

I guess this place collects them.

He was looking at me. I looked back. "What?" I finally asked.

"You're looking for more information about the fae?" he asked. I nodded, not feeling the need to elaborate. "You should talk to Abby."

"Who?"

"Abby," he repeated. "She's a vampire who lives at the Coven House. She's over two thousand years old, powerful as hell, annoying as fuck, and creepier than an animated corpse, but she knows a lot of things about a lot of things. I think she knows about the fae."

There was an ancient living in the Coven House? Damn, I could have used *that* information a few months ago...

I sighed and forced myself back on topic. This was as good a place to start as any.

"How do we get in to see her?" Eddie asked. He kind of just jumped in and hijacked the conversation, probably because he didn't like being left out.

"Just show up," D said. "Unless she's out trying to off

herself again, she'll be hiding in the Coven House basement, maybe teaching Cass more about the tarot."

I wondered about 'unless she's out trying to off herself again,' but elected to not ask. I probably didn't want to know.

☾◯☽

Once we were introduced to Abby, I understood what 'creepier than an animated corpse' meant.

Getting to the Coven House was no problem, and I'd done some favors for the fang crowd in the past, so they weren't unhappy to let me in. The lead warden—a tall vampire woman rumored to have been Israeli *Mossad* before she was turned—agreed to let us meet Abby and led us to the basement.

Sitting in the middle of a black-and-purple Persian rug was the body of a ten-year-old girl, thin and pale with long blonde hair tied back in a low ponytail. She didn't look up when we were introduced, instead focusing on the cards laid out in front of her.

"What do you want?" she asked flatly.

"You're a two-thousand-year-old vampire?" I asked, because I couldn't help myself.

That brought her eyes up, and the look was displeased. "Much to my extreme dissatisfaction, yes. I'm also a cosmic joke. Can I help you?"

And people call *me* grumpy.

"I was told you might know something about the fae," I got right to it. I wasn't usually intimidated by anything, but this frail little girl being the most powerful eternal creature in Adelheid was just freaky. And apparently Eddie felt the same, because he was all but hiding behind me. This little kid could probably tear both of our throats out before we could shout, 'Don't kill us, little creepy girl!'

I was suddenly okay with not having known about her sooner. I kind of wished I didn't know about her *now*.

"I know something," she agreed. "But that's not saying much."

"Could you tell us what you *do* know?" I prompted.

She turned back to the cards, turning over two and spending a long time studying each one before she replied again. I knew she was just fucking with us, but given the imbalance of power in the room, I felt compelled to let her and not complain about it. Anyone who knows me knows that's really hard for me to do.

With a purposeful breath—because vampires don't need to breathe, so they do it by choice or to talk—she finally answered, "To ask about the fae in general is simply too broad a question. There are many kinds of fae. They are all secretive. Their distrust of the humans goes even deeper than in the vampires, and the existence of the fae is believed to be far older. They are not of this world." Pausing, she flipped over another card. "Is there something specific that you would like to know?"

At this point, I realized this trip was half-assed. Normally, I was a lot better at my job than this, but I think having my brother around had me a little unhinged.

"Not really," I admitted. "I'm dealing with a rather strange case of what appears to be a fae who lived like a domestic dog, as someone's pet, and then was dog-napped by another fae."

That brought her face back up, and she smirked. It was creepy to look at. "Only a few fae can truly shapeshift. Many can wear their glamour and look different, but it won't hold up under closer inspection, like tactile contact." She paused. "If one fae took another, they may plan to go home. There is a portal, of sorts, between our world and the fae world. Only fae can enter, but you can get to the area. It only opens once every thirty-three days. I'm not sure where in the cycle it is now, but you might want to check it out."

She told us how to get there. We thanked her and made a hasty escape.

❪O❫

Since there is never any time like the present, we went straight to the address she had given us. It was fairly stereotypical of what one would picture a faerie portal to be: set in the middle of the forest, far back from the road.

The spot we wanted was easy to find. It was what environmental types call a 'wolf tree,' which is a giant tree in the middle of a bunch of much smaller trees. As such, it stands out. It means this spot used to be a pasture, with one tree having been left to climb into if the wolves came after you. Then the new forest grew in around it.

This particular 'wolf tree' had gnarled roots at its base, making the impression of a door with a spiral design...you know, if you stared at it until your eyes lost a little focus. Briefly, I wondered if a hobbit lived inside.

Stopping, I nodded to a tree on the other side of the small, vaguely defined clearing. Eddie and I turned into birds and then found a roost to 'stake' the place out in a way cops never could. Not that I liked bird form very much. I could do everything they could, but my balance for clinging to tree branches on spindly legs was not fantastic, so I wasn't the most comfortable as time ticked by.

Like always happens, just as I was thinking about leaving, we heard someone coming through the trees. Our avian heads snapped toward the sound, and we didn't have long to wait before a man—distinctly elf-looking if you asked me—walked into the clearing with a Pug under his arm, paws tied together with some glittering type of rope and a strange strip of embroidered fabric over its mouth but kept below the nose. It was the strangest fucking thing I've ever seen, and that's saying something coming on the heels of a night where I'd met a two-thousand-year-old vampire in the body of a ten-year-old.

Unaware of our presence, the man walked toward the gnarled tree. I met Eddie's eyes, and we dove from our branch, landing behind them. He must have sensed the magic of our shifting, because silent as the morph was, he turned when we did.

Dark eyes switched rapidly between the two of us. "Don't interfere," he said.

"Funny, don't they usually say things like 'who the hell are you' before that part?" Eddie asked.

I smirked. At least we had the same sense of humor. "I'm afraid we might have to," I said, not sounding apologetic at all. "I don't know what the hell is going on, but I'm here to find out. Really nice old dude is really sad that that dome-headed little thing is gone."

Eddie looked at me oddly. The Pug glared at me. I ignored them both.

"She's got to come with me. I'm sorry for the man, but he's safer this way," the fae said. "He's still alive, and I'll keep him that way."

I would say that caught my attention, but it had already been got.

...then something happened. I'm not entirely sure what, which was really fucking embarrassing for me. But the dog got loose. The fae cursed and held his hand like it had been wounded. Eddic and I were caught off guard and looked between man and dog like idiots for a moment. This gave the dog the time it needed to get the fabric off its mouth and start barking.

Apparently, fae magic knows no language barrier. The glamour fell away, and the woman—who looked a lot like the guy—began whispering at the bonds around her wrists and ankles. I saw them loosen.

"Shit," I spat, my brain finally catching up to my eyes. I dove for her, and she rolled away. I heard the fae man begin chanting in something that sounded like it should be in a Tolkien novel. The woman's binding fell off as I tried to grab her again, but instead of running away, she ran at the man. And the bitch was fast.

Thankfully, I had my brother with me. He was already standing near the chanting man, probably wondering what the hell to do, when the dark-haired blaze came toward them. Shifting to his favorite bear form, he dove in front of her, and she smacked face-first into a wall of brown fur, falling back on her ass.

My cat's paws landed on top of her a split-second later. She jerked her body violently beneath me, but my weight kept her pressed to the ground. Hateful eyes turned on mine, and she spat something in the same foreign tongue the other chanted in. My face began to burn. Roaring, I fell back off her, rubbing at my face with my paws in an instinctual attempt to stave off the pain.

I didn't see what happened next because of the burning in my eyes. By the time the pain subsided enough to even open them again, she was gone. And my brother was loping back into the clearing. When had he left?

"What the fuck just happened?" I demanded, trying desperately not to scratch at my stinging eyeballs.

"She got away," my brother said as soon as he had a human mouth again.

"You are just so fucking helpful." I glared at him. He glared back.

The other guy—who I'd completely forgotten about until then—started stomping and swearing behind us. Now that I remembered him, I whirled away from Eddie and leapt onto this stranger mid-fit.

"*What is going on?*" I growled.

He stared up at me for a moment, blinking as though he'd just realized I was there in the same way I'd just remembered he was.

"Who are you, anyways?" Now he asked.

I blinked, and not just because my eyes still hurt. I wasn't used to getting that kind of response when I pulled out Angry Face. People usually responded with the appropriate level of fear, but he just looked at me in confusion and aggravation.

"Uh..." I was thrown off my game and didn't have a coherent answer.

"We were looking for the dog," my brother supplied.

Trying to regain my senses along with my dignity, I inhaled deeply. "Fae?"

He tilted his head, reminding me of a curious bird. "Very good," he said, shimmering slightly. "The dog, who you could see is not really a dog, is my sister, and I've been hunting her for a while. Thanks to you two, now I've lost her again, and it might be another month before I drag her home."

Confused, I got off him, and we both got to our feet. He prissily dusted himself off. I didn't give a damn.

"Explain." I kept it simple.

He sighed dramatically. "She is my sister. We are both fae. I came to the human world to track her down as soon as I learned she was killing people." He met our blank looks, his eyes starting with me and then going to Eddie before returning to me. I had a jolt of emotion to hear what he said, but I kept it to myself and watched him. There was another dramatic sigh, and I wondered if he was getting ready to audition for whatever latest adolescent cinematic fad was gonna come around. Still, I managed to wait patiently-ish for him to continue. "She pretends to be a dog and gets in with rich people, kills them, takes their stuff, and leaves. Who thinks to look for the dog, right?"

"Mr. Winters," I murmured.

"What was that?"

"Nothing." I shook my head. "So, she's like...a black widow who pretends to be a pet instead of a wife?" See? I was wrapping my head around this pretty quickly, all things considered.

He shrugged. "That's one way to put it," he agreed. "And it's faster and easier than going through with a wedding."

So, she wasn't an idiot. That didn't necessarily make me happy. Stupid got caught more easily than smart, hands down.

"What was that about the month before you can drag her home?" Eddie asked. "We know it only opens every thirty-three days, but how long is it open for?"

"It will only be open until sunrise, so I have to catch her tonight if I want to bring her home to face justice."

I rolled my shoulders uncomfortably. This case was turning out to be more than I bargained for. And I had no idea how I was going to tell poor old Mr. Winters that his beloved dog was really a cold-blooded paranormal murderer. I doubted they made a card for that.

Sighing, I said, "We want her brought to justice, too."

"Then I suppose we have no choice but to work together," he said with more equanimity than I expected. He extended his hand. "I believe this is the human custom? I am Hefin."

I looked at his hand for a moment but then took it. "Dakota and Edward," I returned the introduction. "Are you some sort of...fae police officer?"

He shook his head. "I simply feel responsible to take care of family business and stop my sister from doing any more harm."

That was certainly something I could empathize with. I just hoped he didn't have to see his sister dead to do it.

❨○❩

We agreed that standing in the middle of the forest wasn't the best place to do our battle planning. Somehow, that translated to talking in my car instead. Still not sure how that worked out, but there we were.

"How have you found her before?" Eddie asked.

"Partly, I've followed the news from the local police and used the internet," he said. "I can also sense fae magic and can tell when it's a blood relative. So whenever I have a lead, I go to that area. Unfortunately, until now, I've always been too late and her 'owner' was dead and she was gone by the time I got there."

"So this time, you found her before she killed the man and grabbed her and ran?" I asked. "Effective enough, but not the smoothest of plans."

Hefin smiled wryly. "I know, but it was kind of an impulse. I didn't know when such an opportunity would present itself again, and I didn't want to give her time to carry out another plan."

I exhaled thoughtfully. "Do you know of any place she has in the area that she would go to? Does she have a home or someplace we can start at?" I almost said a 'hideout' like she was a villain in some kid's show, but I managed to stop myself.

"There is one area I know she frequents, but I have yet to investigate it too thoroughly."

"Why is that?"

He frowned. "I've never been sure if I could get into it without attracting more attention than I wanted," he admitted. "I do not have my sister's skill with fae glamour, and I didn't inherit the shapeshifting, so I cannot so easily pass unnoticed."

I nodded. "And where is this place?"

"Your local dog shelter," he replied with a faint smirk.

☾○☽

As a place that still operates primarily for the human world, the pound isn't open at night except for one person to monitor the phones in case of emergency. Judging from the view through the window as we pulled up, it seemed that it wasn't a thrilling job, because that person was asleep at their desk.

We slipped out of the car, and I looked at Hefin. He licked his lips. "She's been here often," he said. "I can taste her magic. It's enough to know that she's been here very recently."

I wasn't used to being the one following the tracker. Usually, I played the role of bloodhound and had other people following me, but this time, we followed Hefin. I felt in the back seat of my own career, but I couldn't smell fae magic. I was good, but not that good.

It did occur to me, amidst all this, that this guy could totally be taking us for a ride and lying like hell. But for some reason, I didn't think that was the case. I believed him, and as such, we could use his help. So there we were, lurking around the local dog pound, following a guy who licked his lips so often I began to think he was part snake. I was just waiting for him to pull a lizard and lick his eyeball. I wasn't sure if I could take that.

Coming around the back of the building, we saw a small stretch of forest. Seeing what was just past the first few trees, we all stopped dead.

"You gotta be fucking kidding me," I whispered. Nothing

ever happened that easily, except maybe in badly plotted mystery novels.

"Son of a bitch," Eddie murmured, apparently having the same thought.

But there she was, digging a hole.

Eddie and I didn't bother waiting for Hefin, or for each other, before we were leaping into the air and soaring forward. We landed on her at the same time, knocking her to the ground.

I shifted to human and clamped my hand over her mouth. I was not going to let her say anything to get me this time, damn it. She glared at me over my hand, and I felt her moving her mouth, like she wanted to bite me, but I was too strong.

Hefin ran up behind us.

"How do you do that?" he asked.

Eddie and I grinned at each other. "Just a little family magic," he said.

Killer fae chick beneath me rolled her eyes.

☾O☽

With her cuffed and gagged with both my stuff and her brother's special ropes and embroidery in the cargo area of my SUV, we stood outside and talked. "What's the plan now?" I asked Hefin.

"She will face the laws of our people," he replied. "There is an hour till sunrise, so we can just make it back, although I do fear my people will not have the same reverence for the lives of your people as I do." He smiled apologetically. "Most fae are not fans of humanity."

"Who is?" I snorted, but then thought about this for a moment. "Why don't you leave her here?"

What followed was a very boring conversation about the human legal system, so I won't get into it. He wanted assurance that she would be punished. And that we were capable of holding her. A good chunk of taxpayer money had gone into making sure jails could hold the paranormal after Cameron's Law. I said I'd see to it as best I could, but that if she was going to go free, I'd hog-tie her and throw her through the next portal to the fae world myself. This seemed to appease him.

"And it will just kill her pride to be kept prisoner by humans," Hefin mused. He looked through the back window of my car. I guess Sis could hear us, because she was glaring daggers. But apparently, her magic was only by spoken word, so a look wasn't enough.

A deal done, I took her to the cops and all but dropped her in Vance's lap. He was confused until I explained, and then he was appreciative. Even if it meant more paperwork. Then we said farewell to our very brief-lived partnership with the fae named Hefin, dropping him off at the forest just before sunrise.

❰ ◯ ❱

The next day, I had to wrap up the case.

I pulled up in front of Mr. Winters' house and got out of my car, pulling out the perky Boston Terrier mix I'd gotten from the pound that morning. The thing was wall-eyed like you wouldn't believe and had a tongue that didn't seem to properly fit in its mouth, but that gave her the look of a perpetual goofy grin. For some reason, it endeared me to the little mongrel, and I had a feeling it would endear her to Mr. Winters as well.

He answered the door and looked wary when he saw it was me. I didn't take it personal because I got that look a lot.

"I'm afraid I got some bad news," I told him.

He invited me in, and I told him what happened. I told him the truth, but I tried to keep it as brief as I could. No reason to make him feel bad, I figured, because he looked like he felt pretty bad anyways.

Sitting across from him yet again, I felt pretty awkward. I nodded at the goofy little dog beside me. "This is Maui. I didn't name her. But she's pretty nice." I faltered here. It wasn't my strong suit. "I thought...you know...maybe you two would...hit it off?" I sounded like a broken machine and stopped before I made a *total* ass of myself. I had to live with the partial.

With a surprised smile, Winters looked at the dog and held a hand out to her.

Instead of just sniffing it or even licking it, she leapt vertically off the ground and practically levitated into his lap. I've never seen anything like it, and for someone like me, that's really saying a lot, but this had been a case full of surprises. She bounced in his lap, licking the skin off his face. He tried to ward her off at first but then was reduced to giggles—yes, giggles—as he pet her.

"She's lovely," he said, trying to avoid getting a tongue in the mouth. "This was very thoughtful of you, Ms. Dakota."

"Just Dakota," I corrected him, smiling. "And I promise, she's all dog. No funny paranormal smells anywhere."

He smiled at me with such gratitude, I swear my four-hundred-year old ass nearly blushed.

After I was subjected to two cups of tea and a discussion of why a Boston Terrier might be named Maui, as well as all his new plans for things to do to make her feel at home, and a promise of a date for my next visit, I finally escaped. But, you know, I hadn't really been trying that hard.

Of course, when I looked at my car, I considered going back in. Eddie was leaning against the passenger-side door with his arms crossed and know-it-all smirk on his face.

"Why won't you just leave me alone?" I whined like a twelve-year-old as I walked around him and got to the driver's side.

"Because I'm your brother," he replied, getting in beside me. "Besides, it's fun hanging out with you."

I looked at him like he was nuts, because he obviously *was*. "How can you say it's fun?" I asked. "All we do is fight, and you yell at me."

He grinned. "Isn't that what brothers and sisters do?"

Taking a moment, I considered this. And then I laughed. "Okay, maybe," I consented, starting the car and pulling off onto the road.

Maybe having a brother wasn't so bad.

Or maybe I'd just have to work harder to get rid of him and get a dog instead.

I'd figure it out later.

SHELTERED

Timeline: This story takes place both before the series begins and some time after *Written in Blood*.

A few years ago, I spent eight months as a bullmastiff.

Why was I a bullmastiff, you ask? Well, basically, I had chosen to travel in that form for a time because I liked it. I like the breed, and when you're a shapeshifter of the sort that I am, why not run with it? (Literally.)

See, I'm the kind of shapeshifter that annoys other shifters, because I can be any animal or human form that I want. My changes also aren't as messy as other shifters. I don't even tear my clothes, which is pretty great, right?

Anyways, I was running around as a bullmastiff in the town of Dawe's Valley, Alabama. I tried to keep myself off the street so that I didn't attract undue attention as a dog running around alone, but I guess I wasn't good enough because I got caught. Animal Control was called by someone, and they came after me. If I'd had a straightaway, outrunning them would have been snap for a preternatural, but they cornered me. Unluckily for me, they were good at their jobs. And this was a couple of years before Cameron's Law, which made preternatural creatures legal, so unless I wanted to 'out' myself in front of these lovely people, I had to go with it.

Besides, what could it hurt? I'm strong and quick, so I was sure I could escape once no one was looking.

Not wanting to be tagged as a 'trouble' dog, I kept calm and went with them. They got me on a catch-pole and loaded me into a crate. I didn't like it, but I tolerated it with a sigh while they talked about how good I was and how I must have been someone's pet because despite my lack of collar, I was being really well behaved. Clearly, someone had trained me. If they only knew, right?

I had never been in an animal shelter before, but given the day and age, I was of course aware of them. Still, it doesn't really prepare you for walking down that long cement corridor with its kennels filled with barking dogs. And man, they went bat-shit when they saw me passing by them.

See, people write animals off as stupid, and they don't have certain sorts of intelligence that humans do, but they know things people don't: like when an animal isn't really an animal. They can smell the supernatural on me, and they don't trust it. Am I a threat? I'm powerful. They can tell. With senses that humans can barely conceive of, they know my strength but don't know what to do about it.

I was released into an empty kennel toward the back. They didn't know how I would be with other animals, so they didn't want to put me with another dog yet. It was smart.

With my super special hearing, I listened to the Animal Control guy talking with the shelter staff out front.

Where was I found?

No collar?

What type of dog?

Was I aggressive?

Heaving a sigh with my canine shoulders, I just let the other dogs bark while I lay down and rested my chin on my paws. I figured once it was night and the workers had gone home, I'd have my chance to bust out of there.

I heard the Animal Control guy go, and a woman came back to the kennels. I hadn't really noticed her as I was being brought in, but I heard her as she made her way to me. She was obviously coming for me, but it took her forever because she stopped at every kennel to help calm the dogs down from the fact that I'd gotten them riled up. Now I felt a little bad about that, but what could I do?

Finally, she got to me and knelt to be closer. She made herself smaller, so she'd be less of a threat to an animal lying down. There was a clipboard with paper on her knee.

"Aren't you a pretty one?" she asked with a flashing smile.

Funny, I was just thinking the same thing about her.

She wasn't pretty like most people thought of pretty. There was a unique look to her face, where there were features that individually weren't necessarily attractive but when they were put all together, they worked very well. Her skin was this beautiful dark brown. I'd make some kind of chocolate comparison, but I wonder if that's somehow offensive. But then, she was delectable with that gentle, kind, pretty expression and gleaming smile.

"You look in much better shape than most of our strays," she said, tilting her head this way and that to look me over. I lifted my head so she didn't think I was despondent, and so I could see her better. The move made her smile bigger, and I felt rewarded. "I'll bet they're right. You must be someone's pet. I'll post you on Facebook and maybe see if someone recognizes you."

No one would, of course, but I appreciated her effort. If I had been somebody's pet, such kindness might see me home again.

She carefully put her hand against the chain-link, and I leaned forward to lick it, doing something I certainly wouldn't have ever done at any other time, but I couldn't help it with her. I wanted her to like me.

I was rewarded with another smile. "You're sweet, too."

She held her hand there for a moment more before pulling back to write things on the paper I couldn't read from that angle. "I'm going to name you...Edward."

Edward? Really? I didn't see where that came from, but hell, why not?

"It's almost dinnertime, pretty boy," she said, getting to her feet. "We'll let you have your own place for the night before evaluating if you can be in with the others. Hope you're good with other dogs, 'cause we can't afford the space to let you have your own room for too long." She sighed so heavily her shoulders visibly rose and fell. "Probably have another in tomorrow, if not more." She started walking away. "Knowing our luck, someone will find another litter of puppies at the dump."

There were sadness and defeat in her voice that got to me, and I watched her down the aisle as far as I could.

She needn't worry, I thought at the time. I planned to break out after dark, so she'd have a free kennel.

❪○❫

Dinner came and went. Dog food is atrocious, thanks for asking, but I ate it all because I didn't want any extra attention. Well, I did want extra attention from her, but I knew it wouldn't be wise.

She seemed to be the only one there that night, and it was late by the time she finished taking care of everyone, locked up, and left. I listened to dogs whine and bark and play with one another before, one by one, they all quieted down. I took that opportunity to shift into human form. The dogs in the kennels nearest to me all jumped up, but only one barked and shockingly didn't set off the rest.

This next part is really embarrassing, so I don't plan to tell you. The summary is that that place was a hell of a lot harder to get out of than I expected. In fact, I couldn't get out. The only way I could was to blast through it, somehow, with a feat of superhuman strength. But that would mean damaging the building. I didn't want to do that to this place or the people who worked there and animals that lived there. I could be a bastard, but I wasn't that much of a bastard. I shifted back into my canine form and waited for morning.

I'd just have to find another way out.

❨O❩

The pretty one was back the next day, bright and early. This time, there were some others with her. Had to be volunteers, no shelters like this were funded enough for that many paid employees, if any at all.

From my lonely little kennel at the end, I watched her as she made her rounds and took care of the animals. She seemed to genuinely enjoy speaking to each one, and they really seemed to like her. Small differences in behavior most humans didn't notice—though some could sense—were easily perceptible to me, given how much time I had spent as an animal over the past four hundred years.

I felt an odd quiver of anticipation in my stomach as I watched and waited for her to get to my kennel. I wanted to hear her voice again, 'cause she had a very pretty voice. It was soothing, like she spent a lot of time calming scared animals. I wasn't scared, but I still wanted to hear her speak.

"Hey, boy," she said as she reached me. "Spend an okay night?"

Feeling pathetic even as I did it, I licked her hand through the gate again. She laughed and held her hand for me.

"Aren't you sweet," she cooed, tilting her head. "I love bullmastiffs, you know. I'd take you home myself, if I could."

Well, now, there was a thought.

Feeling playful, I flopped down and rolled over on my back. My bully breed face gaped open in that goofy grin certain breeds of dogs seem to naturally have, and it made her laugh. "A joker, are you? People do love a dog that can make them laugh." But then the smile faded, and I knew what she was thinking.

I'd probably be hard to get adopted, like a pit bull. Not that I was aiming to get adopted of course, I just wanted out, but I saw the thought clearly in her mind. And it made her sad.

I was just some dog that Animal Control had brought in the day before, but she already worried about what would happen to me. Something deep down melted a little, and I stared at her. She seemed to recollect herself after a moment and met my doggy stare, and a strange look passed over her expression.

"There's something so..." She paused. "It's almost like I'm looking at a person."

Whoa. Perceptive. I'd have to watch myself.

Looking disconcerted by what she had seen and felt, she frowned a little. I rolled back over and just sat quietly as she stood and moved on. I tried not to feel disappointed, because I knew she must have other things to do and was probably a little freaked out.

But I was kind of disappointed anyways.

☾O☽

Days turned into weeks. She came to talk to me every day. She was the one who took me for walks and played with me. They took my picture and posted me on the internet to find a home, which was worrisome. But no one ever came for me.

I was put in kennels with other dogs. They (the dogs)

weren't happy about it but didn't freak out too badly. More dogs came in. Some went out.

Her name was Lorelei, I got to learn, and I thought it was such a lovely name. That didn't surprise me, of course. She scratched my ears in a way that actually felt good. I wondered if it would feel as good in other forms...

I really came to enjoy her visits, because while she spent what little time she could with me, she liked to talk. She figured she was just talking to herself, since I couldn't reply, but I was listening. I learned she was one of only two paid staff at the shelter and helped coordinate the volunteers. She worked a lot. She loved all mastiff breeds. When she was younger—even though she was only thirty-six then—she had wanted to be a veterinarian, but her grades weren't good enough to get into veterinary school, and besides, there'd been no money, and the debt frightened her. She became a vet tech and still did that part-time. I couldn't see when or how, with her seeming to be at the shelter all the time.

Her favorite color was green. (Funny, it became my favorite color too, every time she wore it.) And she didn't like most southern cooking, even though she had been born and raised here in Alabama. She had started down toward Mobile and moved upward over the course of her life. Her father still lived there. She didn't know where he mother was. No siblings, which I thought was a good thing for her in some ways (given my tragic history) and sad in others.

She was really as kind and giving as she had seemed that first night. Every day was pretty awful until she showed up at my kennel.

I kept trying to get out, but the results were the same, and I still refused to damage the building. And I guess my attempts got less over time, because I didn't want to leave her. She would be so sad if I vanished, and I'd already disappointed women important to me enough for one lifetime. Even a life as long as mine.

So I stayed, and weeks turned into months. Sadness crept into her eyes, increasing with each visit. I began to understand why: the shelter was filling up.

This shelter euthanized dogs that had nowhere else to go, and I was becoming among those that had been there the longest. I wondered how long I had. I wouldn't let them kill me, obviously. In fact, I'm not even sure they could. The drugs used to kill the average animal probably wouldn't work on my unique physiology. Even so, I didn't plan to find out. I'd take drastic measures if I had to.

But, you know, I had to wonder. Why didn't anybody want me? I was pretty and really well-behaved. They had no idea how well-behaved I was, damn it. I was a pure breed and very healthy...so why was no one coming for me? Was I too big? Did I scare them? Maybe no one knew how to handle me.

If I thought about it too much, it made even me sad. And I wasn't a real dog!

I couldn't exactly keep track of time as a dog, not easily at least. I knew it had been months, though, and quite a few at that, but I was pretty sure it was short of a year.

Lorelei came to the kennel and knelt in front of me. I licked her hand as usual, but she wasn't opening the gate. She smiled, but it was forced, and I could see the redness in her eyes. Like she had been crying. Who had made her cry? I'd kill them. A woman like her should never be made to cry.

"I'm not going to let them kill you, Edward," she whispered, fingers tightening around the chain-link so hard the skin paled. "I know I shouldn't, but I can't help it. You're coming home with me."

My ears perked up. This would be my way out. But... going home with Lorelei...

As her dog.

This was a mess.

☾○☽

She took me home that night. It turned out that everything about her was little and cute, including her car I was too big for the backseat of. I realized then how funny it must look for her to walk me, but I would never give her any trouble. We crossed the span of Dawe's Valley, which like most towns around here was big and sprawling. There were a lot of fields, some filled with cotton, and I realized it had to be more than six months since I'd been caught by Animal Control.

Her house was little and cute too. One bedroom and built in the era of houses that were made small. Again, not really made for a dog my size, but her heart had been too big.

Yeah, she really shouldn't have taken me, but I guess my death warrant had come down the line.

I moved very carefully through her things, found a nice open space in the kitchen, and curled up. It was the best place I could see to be out of trouble while she did whatever it was she needed to do.

"Home, sweet home," she said with a weak smile. "Just try not to break anything, okay? I won't really be able to afford to replace it, since you're gonna need to eat and all."

And now I was a financial burden. My ears dropped further and further. I was just going to be trouble for her. I didn't want to be trouble for her.

The idea of being here with her was so tempting, even if I had to be a dog to do it, but I couldn't do that to her. No, I had to leave. I planned to escape that night, because it would be better for us both. In the long run.

☾○☽

Once she was asleep, it was easy. I became human, unlocked the door, and left. I didn't want her freaking out about dematerializing creatures, so I left the door open so she'd know how I got out. But I stayed in the trees near her house to make sure that no one took advantage of the open door.

Once morning came and I saw her approaching my breakout, I ran off fast. I couldn't bear to see or hear her reaction.

☾O☽

It did no good. It was bad enough I couldn't stop thinking about her, but I could live with that.

I stuck around Dawe's Valley for a while, for some reason, but I stayed in a human form so I didn't have a repeat visit to the shelter. It had been about four days when I saw it, stapled to a telephone pole: a Missing Dog picture, printed with a photo taken at the shelter.

"Missing Dog: purebred Bullmastiff, approximately three years old, very friendly, wearing a red collar and answers to Edward. Please, if you have any information, call this number."

My heart sank right down to the bottom of my feet. I envisioned her shouting my name into the early morning. Had she cried? She'd probably cried. I pictured her red eyes and sniffling and using what little time she had to put photos on telephone poles.

Oh, fuck.

I withstood it for twenty-four hours. I knew it wasn't a good idea to go back. She was sad now, but she'd get over it. Eventually. I knew that. But I couldn't stop thinking about her. The guilt was eating a hole in my stomach with every passing moment. Every time I started walking, it was like my feet were drawing me back to her house.

Around eight o'clock the next night, I was standing across the street, staring at her little house with its little yard. Too small for me in the form she knew. The food bills. The vet bills she'd spend money on when she didn't really need to... And yet I couldn't leave. My little doggy foot was traitorously scratching at that back door before I could stop myself.

I heard her footsteps. She must have known it was me because they came running, like tiny little beats of thunder, and then skidded in front of the door, flinging it open. She gasped and threw her arms open, and I shamelessly bounded into them. I knocked her back on her ass, but she didn't seem to care. I licked her cheeks and eyes, knowing it was the closest I could ever come to kissing her, but it was enough.

She was smiling. I had made her happy. I had come back to her.

☾O☽

We watched TV. I didn't really fit on her couch, so she pushed away her coffee table and sat on the floor with me. I had my head across her lap and was actually falling asleep as she scratched my ears.

I woke with a start at a banging on the door. Lorelei tensed and bit her bottom lip. She didn't look...uncertain, precisely. It was like she knew who was on the other side but was unhappy about it.

"Stay," she commanded softly, sliding out from under me. I sat up but remained where I was and watched. I was tense now, though.

She opened the door, and a big brute of a guy stood on the other side. "What took you so long?" he groused, not even waiting for her reply before stepping around her. The house wasn't big enough for him either, really. He didn't seem to care, knocking into a little table beside the door. Lorelei caught the vase on it before it hit the ground. He looked like he was about to say something, but then his eyes landed on me and a dark cloud descended. "What the fuck is that?"

"It's a dog, Dwight," she said tiredly, although some sarcasm was hard to miss.

His head snapped around. "Don't get like that with me," he said. "You know I hate dogs. Bad enough you spend all your time at that damn place, but you know I didn't want you bringing it home."

She didn't reply. Kind of just…folded in on herself. His character was clear, but she'd been with him for a while. She had that look about her; that she was used to his beating her down.

"Are you going to fucking reply?" he demanded.

I felt every hackle slowly rise on my back.

"They were going to kill him," she said meekly, arms protectively wrapped around her chest.

"So? Dumb bitch, just let them gas 'im. Too damn many dogs anyways."

I barked. I couldn't help it. I couldn't help a lot of things around her. I was on my feet when he turned his ire to me, briefly. "Better not fucking bite me."

"Just calm down and he'll calm down," she pleaded. She looked at me. "Down, boy, please." At the look in her eye, I stayed put. It was an effort.

"Get rid of him," Asshole—Dwight—said.

"No."

His brows rose. "What?"

"I said no," she repeated. "He's my dog now. You don't even live here. What does it matter to you?"

The look on his face was priceless, like he had never expected that response. Then the darkness deepened. In an instant, the back of his hand careened into her face and sent her staggering to one side. Just as fast, I vaulted over her hunched form and landed on his chest. He stumbled back at first, and then the weight of my large body sent him sprawling into the dirt outside.

The animal in me snapped and growled, really wanting to bite him. I didn't, however, because I didn't want any evidence. I shifted to human, and his eyes widened. All the anger bleached out to terror.

"What the…"

"Don't ever come here again, or you'll find out what I am in the most painful ways possible." I barked at him and then slammed my very hard forehead into his. I heard Lorelei coming around from her disorientation, so I moved fast to toss him into his truck. I was rushing back to the yard and about to shift back to dog—no, as a matter of fact, I hadn't really thought this out—when she was on the front step, staring at me with shock.

"Who are you?" she asked fearfully.

"Uh…" I stammered.

"Well?" she half-demanded and half-squeaked. Then she looked around. "And where's my dog?" Concern took over.

I swallowed hard. "You wouldn't believe me if I told you."

The porch light was full upon me, but it obscured the world around us. There was no one but her and I, and she stared into my eyes. The fear was leaving, and recognition crossed her gaze, but she didn't understand it.

"Try me," she said softly.

I knew I shouldn't tell her.

"I'm Edward."

Her dark brows rose. "You're my dog." The usual disbelieving voice.

I smiled weakly. "Give me a chance to explain before you call the men with the torches and pitchforks, would you?"

Lorelei didn't say anything, but she seemed...open to listening. I took a step closer, so she could see me better, but kept my hands up in a non-threatening way. "I'm not really what you thought I was," I began, looking around. Seeing and smelling no one but her unconscious, newly axed ex in the truck, I turned back to her. "But I can look like it." I shifted back to the dog she knew.

A scream was swiftly swallowed on her part, and I admired her for that. Her eyes were wider than I ever thought a human's could be, but she didn't run away. I slowly padded toward her with my head lowered, and she knelt down to look at me closer. After several long minutes and me in my best submissive posture, she stood.

"Come inside. I think you have a lot to tell me."

☾O☽

Fast forward a few years. I'm now in Adelheid, CT, living with my sister. Having gotten a lead on her and getting up the courage, I'd gone to her with a very important apology centuries in the making. And she had accepted me, sort of.

Dakota dropped onto the couch beside me. "You look like someone shot your puppy," she declared in her usual graceless way. "Thinking about your Southern belle?"

"If you must know, yes," I admitted like the petulant brother I was. "I don't know what to do. I miss her so bad my teeth hurt, in any form, but she doesn't want to leave the shelter. The need is greater down there than up here, and she wants to be where she's needed. And so do I. You need me." Dakota snorted, but I kept talking before she could start. "And I need you. We're the only family we got left, Anneliese, and I don't want to lose that. But God above, I want to be back with Lorelei. And I know she misses me too. She always has that ecstatic heartbroken thing going on when we talk." I sighed. "I'll keep flying back and forth if I have to, but the times in between…"

"So get her up here."

I frowned. "Did you not hear anything I just said?"

She returned the expression. "If you'd learn to not interrupt," she said, just as petulantly as I had earlier, "then you would hear me say… Why don't we buy a big piece of land here? It's green and beautiful here when it's not snowing. If there's less need up here, then you could make a rescue. She could bring the animals up here from down south and work her adoptions from here."

"I didn't do too well at the savings thing. I don't know if I can afford that, and I sure as hell know she can't," I said, even though the idea sounded *awesome*. Who knew that Dakota would be the one to come up with it?

"I do," she said matter-of-factly. "I make good commissions on my hunts, and you can tell I don't buy nice houses or cars." That was a fact.

"You'd do that for me?" I asked, unable to put my brain around it. We'd been back together for a few months now, but after hundreds of years apart, family took getting used to.

She looked at me and smiled. It was one of those smiles she almost never used nowadays. Before my eyes, she shifted her physical form from the human face she preferred these days to an adult version of the girl she used to be. Her blonde hair was loosely braided over her shoulder, and blue eyes glimmered with such genuine warmth that I didn't think I was looking at the same woman who usually scared small children, chased livestock, and offended the public at large on a regular basis.

"Of course I would," she said. "You frequently piss me

off, and sometimes, I want to tear your fucking throat out—"
Oh, there she was. "—but you're my brother, and I love you more than anything on this planet. If handing over some of the money sitting in my bank account could do something to make you happy, why wouldn't I? It's money. I might not seem like it, but I actually do know what's important."

I hugged her so tight that her preternatural vertebrae cracked, but she didn't complain. She didn't hug me back either, but she really couldn't. I had her arms pinned.

"I have a phone call to make," I said with a grin.

And barked happily.

FOREVER

Timeline: This story takes place concurrently with *Bloodshot*.

Never assume anything, or else you make an ASS out of U and ME.

It sounds stupid, but it's really true. And not following this damned cliché almost ruined my life. As a vampire, that's a very long time to ruin.

Consider this story the other side of a coin. Vance has already told you what happened to him, and now I want to tell you what happened to me during that time. I'm sure you've already guessed who I am. I'm Sadie Stanton-Johnston, and this is what happened over the course of a few of the worst nights of my life: when Vance was kidnapped by the Blackwood crime family, and I didn't know if I'd ever see him again.

((O))

I'm going to start with the fight. Up until the knock at my door, it had been like any other night. I had been in the office and then I went home, waiting for Vance to come by after work. There was that knock and I knew it was him, so I hurried to greet him, but as soon as I opened it and saw his face, I knew something was wrong. So unimaginably wrong.

"What's happened?" I asked. Fear struck through me

like lightning. I took his hand and led him to the couch.

"I've got an assignment," he said, then hesitated. He stared at my face like he thought it would be the last time he'd see me, and the fear just hurt worse.

"An assignment?" I repeated, hoping to get him to continue. The strong lines of his cheekbones seemed even starker as his angled jaw worked hard with his obvious anxiety, so strong it seemed like his emotions were bleeding down the walls.

"I'm being sent undercover," he finally said, looking away. He sighed, frustrated, and rubbed at his neck. He always did that when he was disconcerted. "Sam and I leave tomorrow, but I can't tell you much more than that, I'm afraid. I'm not supposed to tell anyone, you know…"

I bit my bottom lip. This was bad, really bad. I didn't like it, but what could I do? It was his job. It's what I got for loving a cop. "I see," I finally said. "Is it going to be…dangerous?"

"Yes."

I appreciated his honesty…and didn't, at the same time. I wrapped my hand around his and squeezed as hard as I dared, or could without breaking his hand. He was a shifter, after all, and me a vampire. I was stronger than him. I could only speak my mind and heart, however. "I don't like this. You'll be, you know, careful?"

"Of course." He hugged me tight. I hugged him back.

"Don't die, okay?" I asked, even though I felt kinda stupid saying it. Like death was at the top of his list.

He laughed mirthlessly. "I have no intention of doing so."

We just sat for a while. He couldn't tell me. I couldn't ask. I knew there was more to it, but nothing could be said. Fear had me choked, and I just didn't know what to do with myself. After a time, we did let one another go, but I wouldn't let him go too far and he just started talking.

"You know," he began, moving my hands into his, "this has got me thinking a lot about you and me." I smiled, barely. "About how much I love you and how it's been a great couple of years together."

"It has." I kissed him. "Didn't think I'd ever feel this way about a man again, after Cameron." I really hadn't. Who the hell could've imagined I'd ever fall in love again, after losing Cameron the way I had?

He smiled. I knew he didn't mind my bringing up Cameron, which made me love him all the more. "Yeah. So, it's got me thinking a lot about...well...about forever, I guess you'd say." When he looked down, it bloomed in my mind what I thought he was about to ask, and it blindsided me. It was something we had never talked about, because it was a touchy subject sometimes: the vampire thing.

And for a reason that I hadn't shared with him. I had always felt guilty for not having saved Cameron when he was murdered, because I was too scared to turn someone, but now I was about to be thrown in front of that bus rather suddenly. He was going to ask me to turn him, and it scared the hell out of me. I didn't have time to try to hide it before he was looking at me.

"What?" he asked in a hard voice. The tone added to my fear. Not that I was afraid he would hurt me or anything like that. But I didn't want to hurt someone I loved as much as I loved him.

"I can't," I gasped, shaking my head in panic. "I... Vance, I can't!"

"You can't marry me?!" he snapped.

Oh, fucking hell... I had *assumed*. "What?" I asked. "What'd you say?" Did I hear him right?

"I was just asking about how you can't marry me?"

"Marry you?" I repeated like a moron.

"Is there a fucking echo?!"

I covered my face and moaned, "Oh my god." What in the ever-living hell did I just do?

He threw his hands in the air as he catapulted himself to his feet. "What?!" He just stared at me.

"I thought..." Spreading my fingers slightly, I winced at him.

"You thought what?"

"I thought you were going to ask me to turn you," I spat out the words as quickly as I could.

He stared at me, and I couldn't tell what was going through his mind, but it wasn't lessening his anger any.

"And that would be a problem?" he asked slowly.

"I've never turned anyone before, Vance, you know that," I said, still speaking quickly. "What if it doesn't work? What if you just die?"

"Well, I don't want to die, but... I mean..." He gripped his hair. "From what I understand, you don't have to actually kill me or anything. Just exchange blood, and I die, and maybe I turn or maybe I don't..."

My skull wanted to break apart, different fears now mingling into a rather explosive combination. I couldn't handle it. It's embarrassing to admit now that someone of my years couldn't handle an emotional exchange, but we are all flawed. Meanwhile, he was staring at me almost like he didn't know me. I had never seen him so upset.

"You're saying that spending forever with me would really be that awful." It was a statement, coldly put. Without giving me a chance to say anything, he stormed out. He had never done that before, either.

"Damn it, Vance!" I called after him, but he didn't turn. I got up to follow but stopped at the door. I took a slow breath to try to steady my nerves so I could speak coherently, but when I opened the door, he was gone. I saw that his car was still parked in my driveway, but there was no sign of him.

☾○☽

I won't lie. I was beside myself. I just couldn't believe the evening had gone so wrong so fast. Nearly pulling my hair out, I went back inside and paced around. I got my phone and called Vance, but he didn't answer. I left a voicemail and then sent a text. There was still no reply, so I called again. Same result. I threw my phone on the couch. I'm not sure how much time passed before I tried calling and texting again with no better luck. And a few more times for the hell of it.

I considered showing up at his apartment, but I chose not to. I think because I didn't trust myself to be out and about just yet.

The door opened, and I nearly tackled the person coming in, my primitive brain assuming it was Vance. Good thing I stopped myself or I might have flattened Madison. Before the door was even fully open, she had a concerned look on her face. It grew even more concerned when she saw me.

"What the hell happened?"

I stared at her. "How did you know something happened?" I knew she had known before she even walked in. "Have you seen Vance?"

She shook her head and held up a box. "I found this in the grass, which means that Vance threw it."

My eyes fixated on the box. I knew what it was, but I was almost scared to touch it. But I did. Opening it, I missed tears. I wished I could cry, instead of just feeling that emotional wrenching without true release. I instantly understood all of the symbolism—the dark red heart because I loved his heartbeat and the tiger's-eye because I loved his tiger— because I knew Vance and knew he knew me.

I sat down. But there was no couch and I ended up on

the floor. I didn't care.

"Madison, I fucked things up."

She got me onto the couch and put a fortifying glass of blood in my hands, and I told her what happened.

"Vance never struck me as the type to not even talk it out," she said, clearly confused.

"Anything else, sure," I said wearily. "But something you don't know is that when he was younger, he was engaged to his high school sweetheart. She led him on for years till breaking it all off after she accidentally found out what he was. When she did, she told him she didn't want to spend forever with him because he was a freak, and it hurt him really bad. He left an entire state because of it. I didn't make the connection until he asked if it would be so bad spending forever with him, but… He was so wound up when he got here, then that and recalling the past." I slid my hand through my hair. "I shouldn't have freaked out, but it just caught me off guard."

She hugged me, and I hugged her back.

Dawn was approaching, and I had to go to bed. In my room, I sat down and used my phone to try to call and text again. I stared at the ring and then put it on. I would see Vance again, and we would sort this out. We would make it better. And I'd say yes.

I tried to call again and again until dawn knocked me out and I fell over dead.

☾O☽

When the sun set and I woke again, I was sore as hell from spending the entire day folded like a badly put-away shirt. My phone was still in my hand, and I checked it. No calls and no texts from Vance. Not a damn thing. I was both angry and disappointed. I knew he would be on assignment now, so I didn't call him. I did, however, call Madison. She would be in the office now.

So you can imagine my shock when I heard her ringtone sounding off in the living room. Ending the call, I hurried out.

Sitting on my couch were Madison and Sam, with Dakota and D standing at the door like a pair of bouncers. I felt like I had been dumped in ice water. I knew something was wrong. I just didn't know who to ask.

"Sadie," Dakota began. She always was the bravest, but her using my first name was a huge red flag. As if it hadn't been bad enough.

My eyes found Sam like I was focusing with a targeting scope. "What happened?"

She met my gaze, and I gave her a lot of credit for that, but my vampire senses could hear her heartbeat going a million miles an hour. She was nervous. "Vance has been grabbed by the people we were sent to infiltrate. We don't know where he is now." Getting to her feet, she walked toward me and held her hands out, as if she didn't know what else to say.

"Where were you?" I asked, my voice low and icy. "You're his fucking partner and were supposed to have his back. Where were you?"

"I was just outside the restaurant. There was no sign that anything like was about to happen." She still held my gaze, though I saw her pale eyes drop to my mouth as I felt my fangs descend from my emotional response.

Now, I was lisping. "I thought that was what you people practiced for," I all but growled. "So where the hell were you?!"

Looking pricked, she held up her hands. "Look, Sadie, this isn't my fault that shit went wrong, and I don't want you blaming me —" She didn't get to finish because I hit her.

Yes, yes, I know. It was immature and out of line. She didn't deserve it, and it was bad on my part. I could have killed her. I did manage to regulate myself to not break her neck, but it would be a hell of a shiner. I was being an idiot. I can see that now, and you know, I knew it then, but I just couldn't seem to stop myself.

Fortunately, I had Dakota and D holding me back before I could not-stop myself from anything even stupider.

"Where were you?!" I screamed at her.

"Sadie!" Dakota snapped in my ear, and I knew that the vampire voice had come out. I growled and pulled it back. Sam was getting to her feet, holding her face.

"I'm not going to hold that against you," she said quietly, looking almost ashamed. A cop who lost their partner carried a heavy burden.

I calmed down. "I'm sorry."

We met each others' eyes reluctantly, but some sort of truce was formed, and my bodyguards let me go.

I stared at the floor until my teeth came back in, then I looked at Dakota. "Find him."

Her gaze was solemn as she met mine and nodded.

"Wait," Sam said, "this is police business, and we're on it—"

Dakota looked at her with That Look. (The woman could be downright terrifying when she wanted to be.) "You had your chance. I'm bringing our tiger home."

If it had been any other woman, I might have been jealous by 'our tiger' but I knew Dakota better than maybe anyone but her brother. She loved Vance like he was her family, and I knew what that meant to her. If she said she was going to bring him home, she would do it.

Her gaze shut Sam up, and Dakota was out the door.

"You go too," I told Sam. She pursed her lips in annoyance but nodded, heading out. D and Madison were left.

I was shaking. The trembling was in every corner of my

body. Vance had been abducted by the bad guys. By *very* bad guys. I knew that much from his reaction to the assignment. He had been scared, and he'd had reason to be. What were they doing to him? What were they going to do to him? Did they know he was a cop? They must have.

"Madison," I managed quietly, "I'm not going into the office tonight."

"Of course not," she said.

"You have to." I looked at her. "The business can't fall apart. I can't do it, so you need to. Please."

She looked like she wanted to argue, but she bit her lip. "Alright, Sadie." Getting to her feet, she hugged me, and I hugged her back. Then she was out the door.

For a moment, I thought I was alone. Then I realized that D was still there.

"I'm not leaving," he said before I had the chance to say anything about it. "You've helped me. I'll help you. Besides, don't have any work tonight myself, unless Madison fucks up the office computer again." He smiled a little, and I couldn't help a feeble laugh, shaking my head.

We were both vampires. I was older, but he was bigger. Chances weren't a given that I could make him leave, so it looked like he was staying.

"Fine," I conceded. I sat down, and he sat beside me. I covered my face and sighed heavily.

"If anyone can find him, Dakota can," he said.

I nodded without moving my hands. "I can't lose him, D."

He said nothing, but I sensed a subtle shift of his body toward me. That indicated support, rather than discomfort. He just wasn't a man of many words when it came to heart-to-heart stuff.

"I lost Cameron when he was murdered by those anti-preternatural bigots. Murdered. Taken from me. And now

Vance… Taken…" I shook my head. "I can't lose him. I just can't."

"Dakota will find him," he said softly. "I'm gonna call Cass."

He got up and left the room while pulling his phone from his pocket. I knew he was calling his vampire girlfriend at the Coven House. She was a rare creature. One of the few vampires to turn with the healing ability. She was also just plain odd, but sweet. He came back into the room a few moments later and sat back beside me. "She's on her way."

"Can't handle a weeping vampire on your own?" I said, unable to resist the faint tease. I was a smart-ass to my core, apparently.

"Can't blame me for wanting backup," he returned.

Things started to blur together for me. I kind of tuned out of what was going on around me while thinking about all the terrible things I was trying really hard not to think about. Like when someone says not to look at something and then all you want to do is look at it. I remember Cassandra showing up, and she soothed me just by her presence, because that was part of the healer thing.

I told her about Vance. About the past and the present. About our last night together and the fight. About the future. Fear and hope. She listened. Cassandra's biggest skill is 'active' listening, where she doesn't have to say a damn word but you just keep talking and are convinced she's vividly interested. And she is.

I talked and talked. She replied a little. Sometimes, D put stuff in. I don't remember much of what was talked about exactly. It felt like I was just bleeding all over them, but it helped, and Cass didn't seem to mind.

Eventually, dawn was coming. That meant a vampire pile of bodies in the only perfectly dark room in the house that wasn't the kitchen floor.

☾○☽

When dusk returned with its obnoxious regularity, I woke up and found two other vampires on the bed. It was nothing scandalous, so don't even think it. We were all still dressed and on top of the covers, but it was the safest room to sleep.

They woke just a few minutes after me. As the oldest, I woke first. I thanked them both for their support and then sent them home. I checked my phone. No good news about Vance being found. Nykk called to check up on me. Madison gave me a rundown of the night's work. I called Dakota.

"I'm sorry." She didn't even bother saying hello.

"No leads at all?" I bit my lip.

"I crawled over every inch of the building he was taken from in a very small form, and let me tell you just how much fucking fun that was. Never spend so many hours as an insect, if you can avoid it. Sam is helping me, because her psychometry will be useful. We just have to find the right damn item."

Psychometry being the ability to read impressions, history, and emotions from an object.

I heard a voice from the other side of the phone, but further away. "She hasn't slept since she left your house." I recognized the voice as her brother Edward, who presently lived with her and 'helped' her on her cases sometimes. Which just meant he did his best to keep her from being a public nuisance, but she was my favorite person on the planet right then.

Dakota snorted. "Don't listen to his ass."

"She hasn't!" he called, and I heard a heavy thud, presumably when something hard hit him. Likely in the head. Dakota had good aim.

"Thank you, Dakota," I said softly.

She cleared her throat as if embarrassed. "I'll let you know if I learn anything." And she hung up without saying good-bye. That was her style, so I wasn't offended.

I returned Nykk's call, and then I decided to go to work. Maybe it would distract me. I showered, drank dinner (breakfast), and then went to the office.

That turned out to be a bad idea, really. I couldn't focus on any real work, so only minor stuff got done, and I probably made a mess of even that. When work wasn't being half-assed-ly worked on, Madison was hovering. I'm not sure how long this lasted before I finally ran away.

My next plan wasn't necessarily any smarter. I went to the station to talk to Sam.

See? I was an idiot.

It got worse. How could it get worse, you ask? Well, let me tell you. When I walked in, they let me go into the squad room right away. They knew me there. So, I walked in and went to find Sam. When I did, I found her at her computer. Her and Captain Roy and a couple others, all with horrified looks on their faces. I had no instant evidence, but somehow, I knew this was about Vance.

I came up behind them and saw something really weird playing on the monitor. I didn't fully register what I was seeing at first. It was a lot of cement, and it looked like some kind of weird post-apocalyptic grunge movie, but then I saw a very familiar figure. I saw Vance. He didn't look like himself, though. There was something terrifying in his eyes that made him look like not my Vance as he fought another man. They were trying to kill one another, it looked to me, and that was not my Vance!

"What the hell is this?!"

My voice made everyone whirl around, and Sam looked mortified. Even Captain Roy looked embarrassed, and the ones in uniform just quietly vanished.

"You shouldn't have seen that," Sam declared, closing out the window.

"What was that?" I demanded again.

"Sadie," the captain began, but Sam said, "I'll explain."

She took me by the arm and steered me to a quiet corner. It was only because I let her, since a human had no chance of moving a vampire if that vamp didn't want to move, but I wanted to hear what she had to say.

"I wish you hadn't seen that," Sam repeated. "The people that have Vance... We don't know much, but we know that they make people fight. Like gladiators. I'm guessing to make money off it."

"Can't you use that video to find him?" I asked.

She shook her head. "We're trying, but magic is blocking us." I only noticed then the shiner she had. I can't say I felt all that bad, actually. "I'm still trying to find the right item to help Dakota find him. I swear, we're working on it."

I did believe her, but I wanted to hate her. I wanted to hate someone or something that was right in front of me to hate.

"Can I do anything?" I asked softly.

"Dakota would say pray." She smiled weakly. "Keep your ear to those grapevines that won't whisper to us. You may be able to learn things that we can't. People may want to talk to you more than us."

I nodded. "I will, and if I hear anything, I'll let you know."

Sam put her hand on my shoulder. Her look said she was worried I'd bite it off, but I admired her for doing it anyway. "We're going to find him, Sadie. And at least we know from the video, as awful as it is, that he's alive."

Taking a slow, deep breath, I nodded again. "I know you're right. Thank you, Sam."

I left the station and started making phone calls, but

nothing panned out. I didn't want to give away too much information, though, so my questions ended up being limited. But those I trusted said they would keep their ear to the ground too.

Having walked while I talked, I hadn't given much thought to where I was going and ended up in front of Vance's apartment. Realizing where I was, I entered the building and went to his door. I had a key and on an impulse, I let myself in. Looking around at his austere, masculine decorating style, I felt a deep, aching pain.

So, I decided to walk around and found that while his furniture was all here, much of his personal effects weren't. I knew that was because they were at my house, and I realized just how much our lives had integrated. I wandered around his room, could smell him everywhere, the tiger's scent coupling with the smell of his soap.

Sitting on the bed, I tried to think. I felt dawn approaching as a heavy lethargy in my limbs, and I forced myself to get up and shut the curtains. He'd gotten blackout curtains for if I ever wanted to stay over, but we always stayed at my place. He liked my little set-away house better than an apartment in a busy building.

Dawn came and took me under it.

☾O☽

I knew the moment I woke that I was not at home, which since these days I never went into the daylight anywhere but at home, this left me feeling quite disoriented. I opened my eyes, and it took me a while to figure out I had fallen asleep in Vance's apartment. That brought the rush of everything going on. Sorrow and helplessness settled over me.

Checking my phone, I returned a very worried call from Madison to explain why I hadn't come home and got chewed out for nearly ten minutes for not calling and telling her I wasn't coming home. I apologized a few times and then she apologized for yelling at me at a time like this and…sappy mess. That's all I'll say about it.

No calls from Sam or Dakota, and I resisted the urge to contact them. If they had news, they would have called me.

No one else had called me either. All my ears to the ground brought nothing, but I couldn't really be surprised. I wasn't a cop, or a private investigator, or a bounty hunter, so why would I be able to learn what they couldn't? Just because I was a vampire and a really worried girlfriend…

I wanted to stay in his apartment. Even though he spent little time there now, I knew, it still felt like something closer to him than anywhere else. I wandered through its two and a half rooms: living area, bedroom, and half a kitchen. I looked at what did remain and saw a man not prone to sentimentality. He had a few pictures of him with his parents, some of friends past and present, in frames on the wall.

One piece of artwork over the couch, which I had given to him. It was a contemporary piece by a preternatural artist up and coming in New York.

And yet, for a man who was not overly sentimental, I couldn't help but look at the ring and smile weakly.

The more I looked, the more I realized just how well I knew him, and the more I cursed myself for my reaction the night before he left. If only I hadn't given into panic… I was managing to not panic right this instant, why could I not have let him say what he wanted without assuming?

I knew his parents' names were Harold and Joyce. He was born in St Louis but went to college in Georgia on a football scholarship. He was already a cop when his ex-fiancée became his ex and he moved up here. His favorite color was orange, and he blamed it on being a tiger. He spoke some French, but really quite badly. Liked sweet potatoes but couldn't stand the texture of lobster. All these little details seemed so silly to remember now, but wasn't it things like that that made up a person? A summary of smaller parts?

I put on his favorite CD—an alternative rock group from the '90s—and listened to it while lying on the couch. Yes, I was wallowing. Sue me.

Hours passed before my phone rang and—smooth, cool, collected vampire that I was—just about shrieked out of my undead skin at the sound and then hurried to answer it. It was Sam, and I felt like I could taste my stomach.

"We found him."

I almost choked on air. Before I could ask, she kept going.

"We're assembling a group to go in and get him. Given… everything, we're letting you come, but you stay in the car until we give the all-clear. Got it?"

"Got it," I managed hurriedly. "Meet you at the station?"

"As fast as you can."

I was out the door before a human would take two breaths and rushing back to the station I had fled just the night before. And as soon as I was there, I was ushered into a car and sat in the back with Sam. She was doing…cop things with her vest and gun while she talked to me. I was too distracted by my anxiety to really care about the details. I knew Agent Jackson was driving, but he stayed stonily silent.

"Dakota found the location," Sam admitted, seemingly grudgingly. "I managed to provide some clues once I had good objects to work off of, but I think she just crawled through the entire city until she found his scent. It's an old warehouse downtown. Looks abandoned from the outside but is owned by a front corporation for the crime family who took him and is much more heavily guarded on the inside."

"Do we know that he's…" I trailed off, not wanting to say the words.

"As best we know, yes. He's still alive."

I nodded and let her get in whatever Cop Zone she needed to. I wasn't going to make them regret this privilege in letting me be there. Nor was I going to do anything to keep them from being on their A-Game.

There were no sirens, but they did use their lights to cut through traffic until they got close and then cut those too. When they parked the car, I sat on my hands (literally) to keep myself still. I had to wait. I had to wait. I had to wait.

They rushed off to do their thing, and I had to wait.

It was a year, at least, before Agent Kai—Jackson's partner—came running back out of the building. She yanked open my door with a strength that surprised me from one her size. All she said was, "Hurry."

I took off like a shot.

It passed in a blur, because when a vampire runs, we can fucking run. Cement was all I was aware of before the stairs, which I took a staircase at a time. There was more cement and bars. Cops swarming around the prisoners, but in front of it all was Sam kneeling in front of a prone body.

"Vance?" I called. Nothing. I surged past Sam. "Vance!" I knelt before him, putting my hands everywhere. The blood was sharp against my senses. "*Vance!*"

"Sadie, I think..." Sam began.

"*SHUT UP!*" I screamed at her. I put my hands over his heart, but felt it as it slowed and I wanted to tear my own out. "I won't let him die." Pure emotion and instinct took over at that point. It wasn't even a conscious thought as my fangs descended and I pierced his neck while his heart still beat, however feebly. I drew just enough to begin the process, knowing that time was of the essence. I cut my own wrist and pressed it to his mouth, willing his reflexes to do the work for us.

I clung to him then, while everything went on around me. I curled my smaller body over his big one and felt the last beats of his heart. I sobbed dryly, wishing I had tears.

☾○☽

Eventually, I was able to get someone to move him to my house. My vampire strength would let me do the heavy lifting, but vampire doesn't fix awkward, considering he was still so much bigger than me. Plus, I needed someone else to drive.

Once he was in the house, I sent everyone else away. I would handle this myself. I got him into my room and cleaned off the blood. That was... I don't know how to describe what it felt like to wash all that blood of the face of someone you love, seeing the bullet hole in the forehead...

Anyways. I cleaned him up. I got him in bed, and I sat on the floor. Not really sure why, aside from fear it wouldn't work. Turning is not 100%, after all. There was a risk he would stay dead...

Dawn caught me while I still sat there. I woke up in a pile in that corner and looked at Vance. He was just the same as before, but the night was filling in around us, so it would be now or never...

His eyes opened. I saw them and felt something seize in my brain. I couldn't speak as he squeezed them shut again. I remembered that. Even the dimmest of light is too bright when you first turn.

"You'll get used to that," I said.

He turned his head slowly and opened one eye, looking at me. I didn't move. I couldn't. I was just...afraid. I had been afraid it wouldn't work, and now I was afraid that he wouldn't forgive me for what I'd done.

"What's going on?" he asked, but his voice was getting used to the changes and somewhat slurred. Before I could form the words to answer, his hands were all over his forehead. It had vanished during the day. How had I missed that? I didn't say anything, because I knew what he was finding and some of what he was thinking. Most new vampires go through a similar process.

He opened both eyes and looked at me. We just stared for a long moment before he pushed himself slowly to a seat. Then, he was suddenly gone from the bed and on the floor before me. He was hauling my body against his and pretty much mauling me, but as desperate and sloppy and wild as the kiss was, it was the best thing I had ever felt in my life. I couldn't kiss him back for a moment, shocked, but then I just let go.

After a too short eternity, he broke away and pressed his head to mine.

"You were dying," I whispered, closing my eyes. "I was with the cops. They made me wait till the room was safe and Sam had already found you. You were almost dead. Cold was already in you. Vampires know death, you know?" I had to stop.

"You saved me."

"How could I not?" I asked weakly. "Vance, I..." I felt myself collapse inward. "I didn't save Cameron. I wasn't going to lose you too."

Snatching up both of my hands, he raised them as if to kiss them but then stopped and looked at the ring. If I had blood pressure, I would have blushed.

"Madison found it when she came home that night," I whispered. "I've been wearing it since."

He kissed the ring and pressed my hands to his forehead. "Will you spend forever with me?" His rough voice was quiet.

It was the best thing I'd ever heard. I smiled and leaned my head against his again. "Of course I will. And now, we'll have *forever*."

☾○☽

After that, it was a little bit of Vampire 101, but he knew a lot already just from having been with me for two years. He drank some blood and found it not too awful, and I told him how it all went down. We were both overjoyed to learn that he was still able to shift, since vampires didn't change other preternaturals so I had no idea until he tried. I told him what little I knew about all the rest.

"What about the prisoners?" he asked.

"Many of them were released, and others are being held."

Something happened then that was something I had never seen: he kind of lost it. I had seen him angry, everyone gets angry, (the fight we had), but Vance was no hothead. This happened faster than I'd ever seen, from zero to sixty. "What?!" His voice was so loud with his new vampire volume, I had to wince and couldn't help a very disconcerted look at him. I wasn't an aura-seer, but I could practically see the red radiating off him until he calmed down with visible effort. "Those people helped me in there."

"Only those that were involved with the Blackwood Family's criminal operations are being held while investigated," I had to point out, though I did so cautiously.

"Damn it!" He slammed his fist into the nightstand, and that fist went right through the wood. He winced as he pulled it free. "I promised them all that they wouldn't be arrested if they helped me, and they gave me a ton of information that could get them killed if we don't take Blackwood down. I won't break my fucking promise to them! I don't care if they were guilty in the past. Don't you think they've fucking paid enough after that hell?"

I stood up and put my hands on his chest. "Vance," I said as softly and calming as I could, "we'll go to the police station. They want to talk to you anyways, so we'll go and you can talk to them about your friends. It'll be all right."

His nostrils flared as he forced a deep breath. "Alright."

《O》

We went to the police station. I had to drive, and then rush like hell to keep up with him going in and to the squad room. I came up in time to hear a heated exchange about his friends in the cell and Roy agreeing to free them if their information panned out. I just reminded him wordlessly of my presence to help keep him calm.

I followed him to holding, where he talked to them for a while, and I was introduced, and then he had to go talk to the other cops about things. I chose to stay and talk to these new friends of his. Part of me was curious, and the rest... Well, it was police business. I wasn't going to push my luck.

"So you're the girlfriend," Elena said. A handsome woman with almost vampire-like intensity, except I knew she was human. She smiled. I didn't know her at all, but how tired she looked was very clear. "He talked about you a lot."

"A lot," the little one, Lucia, echoed. "Looks like you guys made up."

I wondered about just how much he had told them, but he obviously had formed bonds with them, so I didn't worry. I smiled. "Well, dying has a habit of helping seal rifts," I quipped ruefully.

"We were glad to see you," the man named Daniel said quietly. Not a small man, but not overbearing in his voice and speech. "It wasn't hard to figure out who you were, and we knew what you are. We hoped you could..." He didn't have to finish that statement.

"We got lucky," I said. "That bullet..."

"It should have killed him instantly," Lucia finished that

one for me. "Before you could do anything."

Words caught in my throat.

Daniel smiled a little. "The gun had a little help going off course," he said, but he didn't elaborate.

Lucia met my eyes and mouthed the word 'telekinesis' and although it took me a little bit to figure what word she meant (I'm not a lip-reader), I understood. Vance had said they'd been drugged, so that must have been some effort on Daniel's part. Just enough to save Vance's life, and I'd be forever in his debt.

"Vance is determined to get you out of here," I said.

"We won't be upset if he can't," Lucia said. "We are just grateful to be out of that place. A prison of the law will have nothing on that..." She sighed, leaning her head against the bars. "I almost hope for it, since if I get out of here... Well, I don't know where to go."

"Shh, sweetie," Elena said, "we'll help each other out. It's fine."

I smiled a little. "What is it you do, Lucia?"

She gnawed on her bottom lip. "I'm an animator."

My brows rose, and my smile became a smirk. "Are you any good?"

"She's incredibly powerful," Daniel jumped in when a blush filled Lucia's tan cheeks.

"I might have a solution to your problem..." I said with a soft laugh.

☾O☽

Several nights of whirlwind later, and life was...okay again. New, different, sometimes odd, but okay.

Vance and Sam had gotten at least a couple of the bad guys—the one who shot Vance, so the really important one to me—and then Vance had promptly been 'encouraged' to take time off. So what were a couple of vampires to do?

We booked tickets to Vegas for a long weekend and getting hitched. Imagine, there I was, nearly a century old and excited about getting married. Some humans half my age were already on marriages two, three, or beyond. My age, however, was the source of much teasing about the fact I had never been to Vegas in all that time.

"How about Elvis?" I grinned cheekily at him.

"How many times do I have to tell you?" He was laughing when he said it. "We are not getting married by Elvis, even if we are in Vegas!"

Madison popped up behind us after the stewardess told her to sit down. "Come on! Where's your sense of humor?" I looked at her like a sister, and she wasn't about to be left behind. I let the soon-to-be-siblings banter a bit while I leaned back in my seat and closed my eyes, smiling.

He played with my ring, seeming to spin it around my finger as a sort of meditation, and I let him. Since his turning, his temper had been...near the surface, and I was doing my best to help him learn his control again. But in the end, it would be down to him.

The plane moved to the runway, and then I felt the powerful pressure against my chest as it got up to speed and lifted into the air. Vance leaned his head against mine and let out a slow breath. "I love you."

"I love you too."

"Forever and ever and ever?"

I smiled and leaned into him, closing my eyes. "Forever and ever and then some."

If you want to know more about the town of Adelheid, the people who live in it, and the lore I chose to use when writing these preternatural species, you can check out my series wiki at wiki.authorkbthorne.com.

About the Author

Born a Connecticut Yankee in nobody's court, K. B. Thorne grew up to brave snow and talk fast.

She started reading when she was three and never looked back, soon frequently falling asleep with a book under her cheek. At eleven, she discovered *Night Mare* by Piers Anthony and entered the world of grown-up fantasy fiction. As you can guess, it was all over from there. She started writing at fourteen, then met vampires as a teenager and the concept for what would become Adelheid (now the Blood Rights Series) was soon born. Mia Darien followed a few years later, and the books were released.

However, K. B. is also a third-generation Trekkie. Somewhere in a vault at Paramount is a very angry letter written by her grandmother when *Star Trek: The Original Series* was cancelled, so sci-fi is in the blood too. Alongside a love of love and an adoration for her first love of epic fantasy.

K. B. Thorne is the evolution of Mia Darien after years of learning and living. She has taken both of those things to become a smarter, better writer with a fresh new face and take on the literary world. Thorne writes the urban fantasy, fantasy and sci-fi, while Sadie Johnston writes the romance.

These days, when she's not desperately trying to find time to write, she works as a freelance editor/cover artist/ formatter and happily lives her unconventional life alongside her very own Named Man of the North and their mini-tank. (Who is, you know, their son.)

You can find K. B. at authorkbthorne.com!

OTHER BOOKS
BY K. B. THORNE

Writing as K. B. Thorne
Blood Rights Series

Bad Blood
Blood and Thunder
Blood Moon
Written in Blood
Bloodshot
First Blood
Out for Blood
New Blood
Flesh and Blood

Out for Blood Series
Bones & Blood

Bellator (Anthology)
Good Things (Anthology)
Ashes to Sunrise (Anthology)
The Shape of Tomorrow (Anthology)
Born of Defiance (Anthology)

Writing as Sadie Johnston (Romance)
Beauty
Help Wanted (with Viola Dawn)
Threnody (with Alastair Malone)
Here, Kitty Kitty (Anthology)
Amor Vincit Omnia (Anthology)
Second Chances (Anthology)

www.ingramcontent.com/pod-product-compliance
Lightning Source LLC
Chambersburg PA
CBHW021113130726
47988CB00003B/1005